Love is
a time of enchantment:
in it all days are fair and all fields
green. Youth is blest by it,
old age made benign:
the eyes of love see
roses blooming in December,
and sunshine through rain. Verily
is the time of true-love
a time of enchantment — and
Oh! how eager is woman
to be bewitched!

THE RIDGEWAY RUBY

The orphaned Clare, with her coppery hair and green eyes, was no ordinary housemaid, but neither was Ridgeway Manor any ordinary household. What was it that Jeremiah Ridgeway had done which had left old Mr. Ridgeway so embittered? Whatever would happen when the captain returned from Nelson's Navy to the home where he had been so ill-treated in childhood? As Clare pondered these questions she little knew what danger and romance the future held for her.

Prudence Bebb
in the Ulverscroft Large Print Series:

THE ELEVENTH EMERALD
THE NABOB'S NEPHEW

PRUDENCE BEBB

THE RIDGEWAY RUBY

Complete and Unabridged

ULVERSCROFT
Leicester

First published in Great Britain in 1983

First Large Print Edition
published October 1995

British Library CIP Data

Bebb, Prudence
  The Ridgeway ruby.—Large print ed.—
Ulverscroft large print series: romance
I. Title
823.914 [F]

ISBN 0–7089–3387–4

Published by
F. A. Thorpe (Publishing) Ltd.
Anstey, Leicestershire
Set by Words & Graphics Ltd.
Anstey, Leicestershire
Printed and bound in Great Britain by
T. J. Press (Padstow) Ltd., Padstow, Cornwall

This book is printed on acid-free paper

To Bob with my love.

The author wishes to acknowledge with thanks the helpful information concerning fire-fighting in the early nineteenth century sent to her by Phoenix Assurance and by Sun Alliance.

1

"I WOULDN'T have believed it," declared Mrs Scorby, pressing the pastry cutter into the dough, "not if I hadn't seen it with my own eyes."

"You saw it yourself?" questioned Clare, realising that Mrs Scorby wanted to be asked for more information.

"With my own eyes like as I said. Pass me the rolling-pin again, there's a good girl. Of course young Jack hadn't any idea what it was but when Mr Hedges saw it, he knew. He said at once, 'Look at that now! He's written to his heir.' If you asks me," said Mrs Scorby, making a wide gesture with the rolling-pin and scattering flour like a snowstorm, "if you asks me, I reckon the poor old man thinks he's done for. You mark my words, Clare Winster, he'll be in 'is grave before the month's out."

"If he is so ill," said Clare musingly, "ought he to be having pork for his dinner?"

1

"If he don't get what he asks for he'll fly into one of 'is rages and that'll carry him off before the captain comes."

"How long is it since the captain was at home?"

Mrs Scorby pushed the cap back from her red face with a floury hand and thought for a moment. "Master Jeremy was fourteen when he left and that must be all of fourteen years ago. I should think he'll be afraid to come back."

"Afraid?" Clare watched Mrs Scorby putting strawberry preserve into the tarts. "But he's been fighting the French."

Mrs Scorby stopped work, put her hands on her plump hips and pronounced, "If you was to give me the choice between fighting the French and fighting the old gentleman, I'd settle for the French. And I'll tell you this," she added, moving one hand to wag her finger at Clare, "I should think the captain would feel the same. I'll bet no Frenchman's beaten him black and blue like 'is grandfather used to do."

"Poor little boy," said Clare softly.

"Well, I don't know that you'd 'ave called him that. He used to come down to my kitchen and eat my pies and cakes. Stuffed himself, he did. I wonder what he looks like now."

Clare spoke slowly. "I can't understand it. I know Mr Ridgeway is sometimes irritable but I wouldn't call him a cruel man."

"Some folks would. Look at Fred Colt. He 'ad a cottage and a cow but the old gentleman took it from him. Mind you, I don't say Master Jeremy was always as good as gold, 'cos he wasn't. I reckon 'e thought if his grandfather was going to beat him anyway he might as well give him something to beat him for. But 'e was too 'ard on the lad and only on account of Mr Jeremiah."

"Mr Jeremiah? That was Mr Ridgeway's son, wasn't it?"

"That's right. He was Master Jeremy's father and I think the old gentleman was always afraid that Master Jeremy would turn out like 'is dad, but why should 'e with a sweet mother like 'e 'ad?"

"What did Mr Ridgeway's son do that was so bad?"

"Now get out of my way, Clare; I haven't the time to talk no more. Haven't you got enough work of your own to do? I should 'ave thought Mrs Panton would give you plenty of jobs. She'll be real busy."

Which was true. Mrs Panton, the housekeeper, insisted that everything must be cleaned as for a ship's inspection. The chimney-sweep was ordered to come and every chimney swept, which brought soot into the rooms and necessitated vigorous scrubbing afterwards. There wasn't a corner that hadn't been scoured thoroughly within a few days just in case the captain should come promptly in answer to his grandfather's summons. It was unlikely that he would dare to linger unless, of course, he was in some outlandish place fighting Napoleon.

He was.

He only got the letter then because a ship bearing dispatches to the admiral also brought mail from England to the squadron. He would have missed it if it had arrived a day later, for his ship was under orders to return to the Channel.

But at the moment when the letter arrived an emergency also occurred, for one of the seamen had been found

4

smoking near the magazines and Captain Ridgeway intended to make sure that this dangerous misconduct was never imitated by any other man. After the miscreant had been punished and the captain had made an appropriate entry to that effect in his journal, he sat for a few moments with a regretful expression on his face. He knew that the young rascal would be bleeding badly now and salt would be rubbed into the wounds. It nagged at the captain's mind. He seldom ordered the use of the cat. Still, the damned fool had risked blowing them all out of the sea. He began tidying his table without thinking what he was doing and the letter found its way into one of the cupboards under the seat beneath the glazed ports of his cabin.

The next time he thought of it was several days later just as he was buckling on his sword. He was about to go on deck; however, he knew the letter to be a private one and there was nothing he could do about sending an answer to it now that they were so far from land. Let it wait an hour. He arrived back on deck where a sailor uncovered his head to speak to Captain Ridgeway; then he strode on to the quarterdeck, the lieutenants respectfully moved over to the lee side, and just then the lookout called, "A strange sail ahead."

The captain's telescope was out in a moment and as a result of what he saw it was many days before he looked at his letter.

By then His Majesty's Ship *Audax* (Captain Ridgeway) was nearing Portsmouth towing a dismasted prize. The hatches were battened down and below them were a number of French prisoners. The *Audax*'s own foretopmast had only just been repaired, the ship's carpenter was desperately busy and even so she leaked badly in several places. Lieutenant Holmes had a deeply gashed forehead, several men had been killed and the bowsprit was beyond repair. The smooth grey-blue of the English Channel was ruffled by a myriad ripples. Against these the black-and-yellow chequered sides of the ship showed clearly although they were battered.

The sunlight entering the windows of the large cabin fell across the captain's shoulder, making his gold epaulette glitter while he broke the seal on the letter. He looked first at the signature at the end of the epistle, then gave a low whistle indicative of his surprise.

The mongrel asleep at the other end of the cabin by the mahogany cellaret suddenly awoke and padded across the floor to the table, sat down beside it and put its head on one side with an enquiring expression. Captain Ridgeway gently played with the dog's brown ear first and then its white one while he attempted to decipher the sprawling handwriting.

"How does the old devil expect me to read this? It looks as though a spider's walked through the ink."

The dog thumped its tail on the floor and Jeremy Ridgeway frowned over the letter. Having finally succeeded in making out all the words, he swore softly.

Old Mr Ridgeway did not receive a reply to his letter until the day before the captain arrived. He was very affronted by this. His butler, Hedges, and Jack, the young footman, bore the brunt of this anger.

Mr Ridgeway got up from his desk

in the library, holding his grandson's missive in a shaking hand. "Did you ever see such a short letter?" he stormed. "It isn't worth paying for it. Anyone would think he was totally uneducated if he can't write more than this. When I recollect all the money I spent on his schooling! Pah! Wasted! Every penny of it!"

He walked stiffly and Hedges moved forward to assist him. "Get out of my way!" snapped Mr Ridgeway. "I can't walk across my own library without falling over one of you." He glanced wrathfully at the letter in his hand. "Do you know what he says?"

"No, sir," answered Hedges respectfully.

"Well, of course you don't!" snapped Mr Ridgeway. He stumbled over a small stool and grabbed Jack's shoulder in a keen grip to steady himself. "I should have thought you could have stepped forward to help an old man," he protested.

"I'm sorry, sir; I thought you said — "

"Don't answer me back, boy! Do you suppose I pay you to stand around and watch me fall?"

"No, sir." Jack's face reddened uncomfortably.

Mr Ridgeway sat down heavily in a large chair and dropped his stick on the floor. He reread the letter in which his grandson expressed in fluent language and with perfect legibility the hope that his grandfather would be well enough to read the letter.

"You'd better tell Mrs Panton to make all ready at once. Captain Ridgeway arrives tomorrow. You'd have thought he'd have had the decency to let me know earlier."

"Perhaps the letter was delayed, sir," suggested Hedges.

"Nonsense! The mails are never late. It's typical of his thoughtlessness. Young people nowadays are only concerned about themselves. Well, go and tell Mrs Panton!"

"Very good, sir."

The housekeeper was delighted and took Clare upstairs to give another totally unnecessary clean to the captain's bedchamber.

"Did he sleep in this room when he was a boy?" asked Clare.

"Oh, no! His grandfather only gave him that little room at the back up another pair of stairs. Kept him out of the way. I have the feeling he sobbed himself to sleep many a night but he wouldn't want anyone to know if he did."

Mrs Panton pointed to a miniature newly hung there.

"I've always wanted to put it up again," she declared, "but I never dared to before, lest Mr Ridgeway flung it out of the window in one of his rages. There now! It looks just right there, doesn't it?"

Clare looked at the little oval painting carefully depicting in delicate colours the sensitive face of a small boy with soft hair, candid eyes and a white frilled shirt collar. His ears protruded a little, which gave him a somewhat poignant look. So that was Mr Ridgeway's grandson.

Work began even earlier than usual at the hall the day that the captain was due home.

A steaming cauldron hung over the crackling kitchen fire and two smoked hams were suspended from the ceiling. Mrs Scorby broke several eggs into a basin.

"I'll make a genteel pudding," she said. "It always was Master Jeremy's favourite and he'll need something to comfort him when he has to sit down to dinner with his grandfather."

In the housekeeper's room Hedges was showing a similar degree of concern. "When the wind's in this quarter Mr Ridgeway's rheumatism is always worse. He doesn't suffer patiently and, if I may be blunt, he's in the devil's own temper. I pity the captain. It's a bad day for him to arrive."

As the hours passed, excitement intensified among the staff but their apprehension grew as Mr Ridgeway showed increasing impatience. "If he's late I shall not wait dinner for him. I'm not going to suffer acute indigestion just because my grandson hasn't learned to be punctual. You can tell them on no account to put back dinner."

"Yes, sir." Hedges withdrew and informed Mrs Panton that he proposed to place some of the very best wine in the dining-room. "It may mellow him and, anyway, the captain will enjoy it."

"Fancy Master Jeremy being old enough

to drink wine!" exclaimed Mrs Panton, thinking of the pale-faced little boy who used to have milk and biscuits secretly in her room after his grandfather had prescribed bed without any evening meal.

Hedges gave her a reproving look. "The captain will have a very discerning palate. All the Ridgeways have."

They had; but old Mr Ridgeway soon realised what his butler intended and ordered him to restore the superior vintage to the cellar. "What do you mean by wasting my best wine? The boy can take a normal family dinner with me. He's not a royal duke."

In the event, the traveller came in plenty of time before the evening meal, although Mr Ridgeway kept country hours.

Jack, set to watch for the arrival of a carriage, gave the first intimation of the captain's coming. "He's here," he announced laconically as a chaise entered the main gateway.

Hedges soon had most of the staff drawn up in the entrance hall. Mr Ridgeway came out of his library. The butler hurried forward to offer his arm.

The old gentleman waved him aside with his stick. "Get out of my way. I can walk perfectly well, as you know."

He made another irritable gesture and dropped the cane on the tiled floor with a clatter. "Well, pick it up one of you! Don't stand there like statues."

Clare gave it back to him while Mrs Panton fingered her chatelaine nervously and murmured, "Poor Master Jeremy!"

Her employer overheard this and it angered him. His black eyes flashed. "Nonsense! He's only coming for what he can get."

The yellow chaise passed the pink rhododendrons, which made a splash of bright colour against the dark background of the laurels in the shrubbery and progressed up the drive towards the house, where the front door had already been opened. Wheels crunched on the gravel as the carriage approached this entrance.

"He's come!" said Mrs Panton and Clare noticed that the housekeeper was trembling and wondered whether it was with joy at the captain's arrival or fear about the reception awaiting him.

Mrs Panton herself was very relieved that Mr Ridgeway had not decided to remain in the library and wait for his grandson to be brought to him there. She had expected that and dreaded it, for the last time he had spoken to Master Jeremy had been in that solemn-looking room and she recalled vividly the white-faced youth walking out stiff with pain while his grandfather trumpeted after him, "Get out of my sight as far as you can go! I don't wish to see you again."

And now Mr Ridgeway appeared to be walking with alacrity down the steps to the chaise. She would have thought he was eagerly awaiting the captain if she hadn't seen the glowering look beneath the heavy grey brows. The squire was in one of his moods certainly.

Mrs Panton gripped Clare's hand. "Mr Ridgeway's worked himself into a rage. I can see it. It was wicked to bring the boy home."

The door of the chaise was opened and the sole occupant leapt out.

"So!" exclaimed Mr Ridgeway. "You've come, have you? Come to see what you can get, eh? The carrion crow hovers over

14

the remains, what?"

Mrs Panton literally hid her face in her hands. What a cruel homecoming! Nothing had changed. How could anyone speak so to his own kin and after fourteen years? She just couldn't look at poor Master Jeremy's face.

But she could hear his voice; so could Clare; so could anyone over a long distance.

"How dare you come down the steps to meet me? It's easy to see there's not much wrong with you. You write giving me the impression that you are dying and want me to comfort you. I've left my ship to come to a healthy, selfish man. Don't you realise we are at war? Do you think I've nothing better to do than come running at your behest? I'm supposed to be fighting my country's enemies. How dare you, sir?"

It would be an exaggeration to say that Mr Ridgeway cringed but he was certainly stunned into silence.

Mrs Panton dropped her hands now and stared fascinated at the face on which Clare's gaze was also fixed, while the old man remained speechless.

Captain Ridgeway towered above his grandfather. His face was not pale at all; it was bronzed, the mouth was firm and straight but in the lean features were the very dark eyes inherited from the squire. Despite the loud voice, which would easily have been heard across the quarterdeck, and despite the tirade, which he had just uttered, there was a decided gleam of humour in the captain's eyes.

Clare looked again wondering if she had imagined this. The captain turned towards her and, remembering her manners suddenly, she sank into a curtsy, gracefully performed despite her position on the top step, where she was waiting to be of assistance if required.

Mr Ridgeway suddenly presented the appearance of a feeble person. He swayed and took a firm hold of Jack but his alert black eyes darted a quick look under their thick brows at his grandson, assessing the effect upon him of this demonstration of weakness as he began to hobble towards the steps. Jack's left shoulder was literally bowed under the weight of his employer.

"You'll crush that lad," said the captain but his voice remained loud and cheerful. "You'd better take my arm instead of his. Extraordinary type of illness yours, isn't it? You were able to hurry down the steps."

"Some sort of wasting disease, I suppose," said Mr Ridgeway.

"The sort that wastes other people's time and energy, eh? I had a young lieutenant like that once on the *Audax*. He was only sent to me because his uncle was an admiral. He was a damned nuisance at first but I found ways of curing his disease."

Mr Ridgeway didn't lean so hard upon his grandson as he had done on Jack. His new supporter trod firmly up the steps and, unknown to the old gentleman, listened intently to hear if his grandfather was experiencing difficulty in breathing. Mr Ridgeway, who hadn't thought of feigning breathlessness, walked up the short flight with ease and the captain disengaged his arm as they entered the house.

Mrs Panton took a step forward and suddenly the picture she had cherished for fourteen years of a pale boy with a pathetic air vanished completely. She had to look up a long way to see the bronzed countenance of the stalwart figure who stood there. She curtsied deeply, her black skirts rustling, and murmured, "Good-day, Captain Ridgeway. Welcome home, sir."

She bowed her head in its white cap so she didn't see the expression in his eyes but in two strides he was across the hall and she felt him grasp her elbows and raise her.

"Mrs Panton! My old friend — though not looking any older, of course!"

He kissed her on each cheek.

A smile covered her face. "Oh, Mast — I mean, oh sir, how glad I am to see you!"

"And I'm glad to see you."

Mr Ridgeway, suddenly jealous of the affection shown to his housekeeper, said snappishly, "Yes, yes, I dare say but Mrs Panton has work to do."

"Things haven't changed here much, have they?" commented the captain, winking at Mrs Panton.

Clare was watching this interchange with

interest when suddenly a wagging canine body hurled itself at her. Instinctively she petted it while two large pawmarks appeared on her white apron.

"Come down, Horatio!" commanded the captain and now his eyes were definitely twinkling. "That's no way to treat a pretty woman! The trouble is that you and I have hardly seen a female for months."

Mr Ridgeway gave a reluctant crack of laughter which he hastily changed into a disapproving grunt.

Hedges was giving orders concerning the bestowal of the captain's luggage.

"I suppose you'd better come into the library for a glass of Madeira," said Mr Ridgeway grudgingly.

"Thank you for the gracious invitation," said the captain with a mocking laugh.

As the two gentlemen went into the bookroom members of the household exchanged eloquent glances of amazement. It was with great reluctance that they dispersed to their various tasks, wondering whatever was being said behind the closed door.

Hedges was more fortunate than the

rest. His position enabled him to hover in the hall and since neither of the Ridgeways was in the habit of moderating his voice, the butler heard much of their conversation.

"You needn't think you're going to keep that dog here," grumbled Mr Ridgeway. "I won't have it under my roof."

"Very well," answered the captain. "I'll go and put up at the Red Lion and take him with me."

"And what do you think people will say about that?" snapped the old man.

"They will say that you turned me out but you needn't worry, I shall tell them you didn't but that I simply wasn't prepared to put up with your ill temper."

"In other words you expect me to house that cur."

"Horatio has been with me under fire and I won't abandon him now."

"Horatio, eh? Called after Nelson, I suppose? I wonder what the admiral would have thought of that."

"He liked the idea."

"You mean he knew?"

The captain nodded. "I was dining on

his flagship when this fellow was born." He gently played with Horatio's ear, a custom the dog enjoyed.

"On terms with Lord Nelson, were you?"

"His lordship was always very friendly towards me even though I was only a junior captain. He was an excellent man to work for."

Mr Ridgeway lowered his eyelids to hide the gleam of pride but he said, "I can't imagine what they called you in the navy."

"They called me Jerry."

"Bah! Your father should have called you Jeremiah after me and himself; but he would break with family tradition."

"Thank God for that! I'm no Jeremiah."

"Well," said the old man thoughtfully "I don't think the worse of you for defending your father."

"It wouldn't make any difference if you did," replied Jerry. "I should still do it."

Mr Ridgeway's momentary good humour disappeared. "I suppose you've been borrowing money on the security of what you're going to inherit from me, eh?"

"No, I've never borrowed a penny. I preferred to go hungry."

Mr Ridgeway gave a snort of disbelief as he recalled the leather trunks being carried into the house and as he glanced at the heavy gold signet ring on the captain's hand and the gold fob which hung from the younger man's waistcoat. "Expect me to believe you're short of funds?"

"Not now. I've had enough prize money to keep me for years. But of course I've been hungry. I was once a half-pay lieutenant."

Perhaps it was a twinge of conscience which caused Mr Ridgeway to say gruffly, "You could have applied to me."

"Not likely!"

Mr Ridgeway disguised his chagrin with censure. He surveyed his grandson critically, noting the brown coat, which was tailored well to his tall person, the white starched neckcloth, the fawn pantaloons and the hessian boots with tassels which swung jauntily as Jerry strode about the room.

"You're as restless as a lion in a cage and I hope you don't intend to sit down to dinner in all your dirt."

"My dirt!" The exclamation was more amused than indignant. "I'll have you know my boots have been polished and my fingernails are clean. Do you want to look behind my ears?"

"There's no need to take that tone with me, lad. When I was a young man we didn't think to dine without changing into suitable clothes. Just look at you! Disgusting! When I go into dinner in half an hour I shall be wearing knee-breeches and the best lace at my neck and wrists. I shall expect you to do the same. I don't know what you young people are coming to. No wonder there's so much vice and immorality these days."

Jerry gave a rueful smile. "I fail to see how a few lace ruffles can preserve me from a licentious life. However, I'll dress for dinner now. I see no reason why I shouldn't please you in this matter." He laid particular emphasis on the last three words and walked to the door from which Hedges had to withdraw rapidly lest anyone imagined he had been eavesdropping.

"We'll meet shortly at dinner," said Mr Ridgeway.

"Yes," replied the captain inexorably. "There's a lot I want to say to you."

Since the last remark was of the kind which might have been uttered fourteen years previously by Mr Ridgeway to his grandson, Hedges gave a gasp which he hastily turned into a slight cough.

2

WHEN Jerry descended the stairs half an hour later no one could have found a fault with his appearance. He wore a blue coat and white knee-breeches. At his throat was a jabot of Mechlin lace in which a solitary diamond sparkled. His black shoes were ornamented with diamante buckles and in his hand was an enamel snuff-box painted with a shipping scene and mounted in gold.

"I presume you didn't want me to wear a dress sword?" he said in that voice of half-amused mockery which Mr Ridgeway was beginning to find strangely disconcerting.

They walked into the dining-room which had been so meticulously cleaned on Mrs Panton's orders. A bowl of deep pink roses scented the whole room, their petals full-blown and curling. The wax candles in the chandelier were all lit and their reflected lights glittered on the glass droplets.

With a flick of his coat-tails Jerry sat down at the rosewood dining-table and demanded, "Now, sir, I want an explanation."

"YOU want an explanation!"

Across the table two pairs of black eyes met and held. It was the older man who dropped his gaze first.

"Very well."

"I wish to know why you wrote me a pathetic letter suggesting that you were in urgent need of me. The implication that you were dying was, as I can see, untrue. I am happy that you are not about to depart this life but I do not care to be summoned away from my duties on what I can only describe as a false errand."

It was almost in the voice of a man who is defending himself that Mr Ridgeway replied, "It is time you learned about your inheritance. The estate will be yours before many years, perhaps much sooner. You know nothing about it because you have been away for so long."

Jerry refrained from saying that his grandfather had been the original cause of that but he looked steadily at the old man. Again Mr Ridgeway shifted his gaze before he continued, "Recently I instigated the passage of an Enclosure Act and as a result we have gained large tracts of fertile land. I shall leave you far more than I inherited, besides all the money in Funds."

"I still object to the false impression deliberately given to me in that letter. However, tomorrow we will discuss the effects of the enclosure."

Mr Ridgeway gave an audible sigh of relief and swallowed some soup.

Jerry lifted his wineglass, which was engraved with a floral design and supported by an air-twist stem, while he looked critically at the liquid it contained. He swallowed some and made a grimace. "Wherever did you get this, sir? Out of the village pond?"

His grandfather, who was uncomfortably aware of the reproachful eyes of his butler, didn't have time to reply before Jerry continued, "Hedges."

"Yes, sir."

"I brought with me a crate of a very pleasant Portuguese wine. Get me a bottle of it."

"Very good, sir."

Mrs Scorby had excelled her previous successes. The white soup, the fish in oyster sauce, the braised ham and roast goose were particularly fine but, as she had hoped, the genteel pudding found special favour with Jerry.

On the walls surrounding the diners were portraits of several generations of Ridgeways. Opposite to Jerry the face of Sir Andrew Ridgeway, knighted by a grateful Charles II at the Restoration, seemed to laugh from beneath its Cavalier curls and plumed hat. The same dark eyes reappeared in the more solemn countenances of Lucius Ridgeway, painted by Kneller when he was a member of the Kitcat Club. Jerry's grandmother, Katherine, the daughter of an earl, showed her patrician features beneath powdered curls. No Ridgeway had ever been ennobled himself, but they had farmed the same ground for generations, before Andrew Ridgeway had fought at the Battle of Worcester and subsequently aided his deposed monarch to escape.

Jerry twisted round in his chair to view the picture which had been his favourite as a child. It showed the juvenile Edward Ridgeway in a blue satin suit with his hand on the head of a Great Dane which sat protectively beside him.

"Where is the portrait of my father?" he rapped out the query.

"Somewhere or other."

"Where?" The word sounded menacing.

Mr Ridgeway couldn't evade the question. "It's in the attics."

"Then we will have it brought down tomorrow and hung in here."

"There's no room for it."

"Take down the picture of my great-uncle and put it there."

Mr Ridgeway glanced at the likeness of his brother the uniform he wore at the Battle of Minden. "The painting of James looks very well in that position."

"Nevertheless it will be moved tomorrow."

"I don't want it moving."

"You will become accustomed to the change."

Mr Ridgeway's fingers tightened round the stem of his wineglass. "Now look here, Jeremy — "

"The portrait of my father will be

hung on that wall tomorrow." It was a command.

"Oh, very well." For the first time in twenty years Mr Ridgeway capitulated to someone else's orders.

Having won his point, Jerry determined to lighten the atmosphere by asking, "What have you got in your stables these days?"

"There's a frisky bay mare which doesn't get enough exercise since I can't ride much. She might suit you. Columbine, she's called."

"I'll try her tomorrow. That's something one misses in the navy — riding."

Mellowed by good wine and pleasantly relaxed by succulent dishes, the two men began to talk amicably about the British fleet.

Describing the dismasting of a French ship Jerry made a sweeping gesture. The prongs of his fork caught in the fine Mechlin lace at his wrist which tore as he wrenched the implement free and knocked over a wineglass.

"Damn!" said Jerry. "This is the last time I'll dress up like this for a family dinner. I'll wear what I want tomorrow and if you don't like it I'll take my dinner on a tray in the library."

The butler left them with a decanter of the finest port and went to the housekeeper's room, where he related *sotto voce* (because Clare was present) what he had just heard.

A burst of laughter from the dining-room caused Hedges to look very significantly at Mrs Panton.

She nodded her understanding. "It seems strange, doesn't it? Somehow I like that room better now. I used to hate going in there for ages after that terrible day one November when Mr Ridgeway was so angry with his grandson you could hear him in the kitchens."

Hedges nodded sombrely but he didn't intend to discuss his employer in front of Clare. He picked up a tray of glasses and walked towards his pantry, decorously holding the tray aloft.

Mrs Panton explained, "Master Jeremy was only behaving like any other healthy boy of his age. You can't tell me he was the first to think of dropping a beetle in his grandfather's glass of wine."

Clare laughed. "Did he really?"

"Yes," said Mrs Panton proudly. "He was always a brave boy."

She liked to invite Clare to her room, for the girl always listened politely but it was time for Clare to return to the servants' hall.

She called in at the kitchen and found the cook still busy but very well satisfied with the reports which had come down to her of the hearty appetite with which the captain had consumed his dinner. Already she was preparing an elaborate menu for the next day.

Clare said, "How clever you are! That looks very appetising."

Mrs Scorby regarded a pie with a golden-brown crust and beamed with satisfaction. "He always liked my apple pies. I think later I'm going to creep up the backstairs and see if I can catch a glimpse of Master Jeremy when he goes into the drawing-room."

"I shouldn't trouble to do that if I were you. He's not really worth looking at," said a cheerful voice.

Everyone turned to look in its direction and there, standing framed in the doorway, was Captain Ridgeway.

His tall figure nearly filled the aperture; he must often have needed to bend his head in the confined quarters of a ship but there was no stoop to his shoulders. He stood erect, the dark eyes twinkled in a face whose suntan was accentuated by the spotless white lace at his throat.

"Master Jeremy!" Mrs Scorby hurried across the flagged floor, her arms outstretched, and then suddenly stopped short of him, sank into an unsteady curtsy and said, "Good evening sir," in her most prim voice.

He threw back his head and laughed, then bent forward and kissed her on both cheeks as he had earlier saluted the housekeeper. "You always were my favourite flirt," he teased. "Haven't you got any bowls or pans for me to lick out?"

He sat on the corner of the strong wooden table and swung his leg. The kitchen candles were only made of tallow but even so their light shimmered on his shoe-buckle.

Mrs Scorby looked at him. It was fourteen years since he had last sat on the corner of that table. She noted that the face which had been so pale in those days was rugged and tanned now. Two tears coursed slowly down her cheeks. She ignored them but when more followed she half turned away from him to remove them with a corner of her apron. A long arm stretched out and caught her elbow pulling her back to face the captain.

"Not crying, Mrs Scorby?"

"No, sir. I've been peeling onions."

"Of course! They were wanted for the apple pie, no doubt!"

"Oh, Mast — oh, sir!" she began to chuckle, caught his eye and discovered that, however tall and strong he had become, the twinkle in those black eyes was the same — no, it was more pronounced than ever.

"Have I to wait until tomorrow for that apple pie?"

"Do you mean you could eat some now, sir?" Mrs Scorby's face registered the amazement she felt, for she knew to her satisfaction exactly how much he had consumed at dinner.

"I could if you would give me some."

"Fetch a dish and spoon, Betsy," said

Mrs Scorby, all evidence of tears now gone.

As she bent to cut a large slice of the pastry, Jerry looked over her bowed head at Clare. Their eyes met for a moment. She thought he had the most attractive eyes she had ever seen. He mused to himself: whatever is the old gentleman doing with such a pretty and ladylike girl for a housemaid? Aloud he said, "That's just right, Mrs Scorby. I could have done with you in the galley of the *Audax*. Salt pork is the very devil, you know?"

"Well, I don't believe that's all you had. You'd stock up with plenty of food for your table at every port or my name's not Annie Scorby."

"Which it is," he said taking the dish and spoon, "and I did manage to keep three bullocks, some pigs and chickens to provide me with more appetising fare — apart from the wine, of course. It would have been a shocking thing if I couldn't give the admiral a respectable drink if ever he should be piped aboard!"

Mrs Scorby sat on a ladderback chair and watched joyfully as he swallowed a large mouthful of pie.

"Very good, Mrs Scorby. You always did put the right quantity of cloves in."

She beamed.

The door opened and Hedges came in quietly. "I thought I heard Captain Ridgeway's voice. Sir, I am so thankful to find you. May I have a word with you, sir?"

"As many as you like." Jerry put his empty dish on the table.

"I wish to apologise about the wine, sir; but I do assure you — "

"You don't need to assure me, Hedges. I know perfectly well that wasn't your choice of wine."

The man's anxious face relaxed a little. "I think you will find, sir, that we have some very pleasant wines in our cellar. It is just that — " he hesitated not daring to explain the truth.

Jerry waved his hand in a careless gesture. "Stop worrying, Hedges. My grandfather thought they'd be wasted on a reprobate like me, eh?"

"Well, sir — " An uneasy frown creased the butler's forehead.

"I've told you not to worry," repeated Jerry whilst a smile crinkled the corners of his eyes. "I didn't suppose for a moment that the wine had your approval. I know that he believes I'm the biggest scoundrel unhung."

"If I may venture to say so, sir, I don't think that is his opinion any longer; not after tonight, sir."

★ ★ ★

Clare couldn't sleep. Every time she was about to slip into oblivion she seemed to see a pair of laughing black eyes. It was most annoying.

Eventually she got up and went to the window, pulled back the curtain and sat looking out into the night. She possessed no dressing-gown but she drew a shawl round her shoulders. It had been intended as a present for her mother, who had died before Clare had finished making it.

Her small bedchamber in the attic storey was high enough to provide a vantage-point over the shrubbery, the drive and even, in clear moonlight, across the road to the barley field which was on the edge of Mr Crewe's property. All the Ridgeway land lay to the south and east of the manor house. If she turned sideways and twisted her neck at an uncomfortable angle she could just see across to the village green on a bright night.

But tonight the only moon was a narrow crescent, although the blackness was pierced by the sharp sparkle of stars.

If she couldn't sleep she might as well do something useful. She lit a candle and went to the solid oak chest of drawers made by a local carpenter and very different from the elegant furniture in the first-floor bedchambers.

She took out a bundle wrapped in a clean but faded piece of cotton fabric, opened it and shook out a white gown, which she had made out of muslin and which fitted her perfectly, although she never expected to wear it, for housemaids did not require such things. Perhaps one day if she needed money, she would sell it. She had added a blue sash to it and all her spare time was spent painstakingly embroidering in white a delicate pattern of flowers on the small sleeves and on the petticoat which showed through the open robe. Whoever wore it one day could feel elegant, for there was nothing fussy about the beautifully executed design of white on white.

She lifted up the mahogany workbox which was the only one of her mother's possessions they had allowed her to keep. There was a little brass neatly fitted into the lid with the name Isabella Winster engraved upon it. The box was divided into many small compartments inside and Clare took out a thimble and selected a needle, but in the scanty light afforded by her solitary candle she could hardly see to thread it.

So she sat still beside the small window for a long time, silently holding her gown and staring into the blackness until that darkness itself began to pale. The first birds sang, the tower of the Saxon church became faintly discernible and then the full dawn chorus began.

Clare got up, wrapped her gown in its faded cover, stowed it in the drawer and gently placed her mother's workbox beside it. She went back to bed for the short time which remained to her for rest.

It wasn't long. She had hardly drifted into sleep before Betsy knocked on the door to waken her. There was no time to waste.

She rose, donned a dark gown, brushed her hair and put on her white cap, tied her apron in position and hurried down the long flights of stairs to get a bucket filled with water. She washed her face in cold water at the pump, then staggered with her heavy bucket to the hall. The black-and-white tiled floor had to be scoured before anyone else came across it.

She washed away the footprints and the dust, rubbing vigorously, and wondered if the muscles in her thin arms would develop as a result of this sort of work. So far they didn't seem to show any signs of doing that.

"Whatever are you doing down there?"

The captain's voice and his firm footstep on the stairs broke through her reverie. She coloured with embarrassment; got quickly to her feet, still holding her wet cloth, and curtseyed.

"Good-day sir. I was cleaning the floor."

"I don't think you should be doing that job."

The flush on her cheeks deepened. "I beg your pardon, sir. I didn't know you would be up so early or I would have finished it sooner."

"Good God! I didn't mean that!" He looked musingly at the girl in front of him. The blush was fading and it left her cheeks very pale, emphasising the scattering of freckles inevitable in one whose hair was liberally supplied with tints of Titian red. She raised her eyes to his face for a brief moment and he saw that he had been right in the kitchen last night; they were green. The fingers clutching the damp cloth were long and slender.

"My objection is that you should be cleaning this floor at all."

"It's part of my work." The pink was staining her cheeks again. How much she had always wished that she did not blush when people spoke to her! Conscious that she was doing so, the blush deepened. Her fingers tightened nervously round the cloth.

It was dripping dirty water; suddenly

he took it and flung it on to the floor. "On the *Audax* I had tough seamen cleaning the decks. Why do I come home and find a young lady scrubbing my grandfather's floor?" He had emphasised the word 'lady' and the flush became painfully vivid. Jerry looked at the slight figure and then at the heavy bucket. He snapped his fingers as the footman appeared at the back of the hall. "Jack, come here! Take that pail to empty it and don't tell me it's not your job."

Clare looked with concern at the captain. Suppose he questioned her about the reason for her becoming a housemaid here?

Jerry regarded her perceptively. She didn't want him to probe deeply. Very well, he wouldn't — at the moment.

She thanked him for the consideration he had shown her. "But I ought to finish this floor."

"There's not much point. My dog will spoil it, anyway."

At that moment Horatio bounded upon the scene. The animal padded across the floor, proving the force of Jerry's argument by leaving pawmarks on the

42

wet tiles. Clare patted the rough hair on Horatio's neck. "He's a nice dog."

"I think so," agreed Jerry, "but I must confess that he has absolutely no morals."

She laughed.

"Come on, Horatio! Off to the stables!" Jerry strode out of a side door whistling 'The Little Fighting Chance'.

The groom, who brought Columbine out for his inspection, did not expect that a man who had spent most of his adult life at sea would make a good rider. After watching Captain Ridgeway rapidly get the mettlesome mare under control and trot out of the cobbled yard he changed his mind.

Jerry took a nostalgic pleasure in galloping over a stretch of grassland where he had habitually exercised his pony as a child. Then he swung westwards, slowing Columbine to a canter and passing the oak tree which had been a landmark during boyhood rides.

It was not far beyond that tree where he discovered radical changes had taken place.

He should have come upon the

common. Instead, he encountered a large field where barley, still green but already tall and whiskered, was rustling in the breeze.

And was that really Fred Colt's cottage? The rafters were bare to the sky, denuded of tiles or thatch. It appeared skeletal. Pink roses still climbed the wall and there was the bush where he and Fred had found a robin's nest one spring, but the door to the cottage was stuck half open, the wood swollen by rains. The garden had gone; where the brown cow used to be tethered the corn grew, for the barley came right up to the back wall of the cottage. For a dreadful moment Jerry thought that Fred might have died but he recalled that the dilapidated cottage was a victim of the enclosure and its owner would be living elsewhere. Standing up in his stirrups he looked farther afield. Narrowing his eyes in the sunlight he nodded comprehendingly. Yes; that large barley field and the field beyond it were now part of his grandfather's property. There could be no doubt of that, but where was Fred Colt?

He turned northwards and rode between

wide verges where cow parsley, dock and tall stems of sorrel straggled near the ditch. On the other side of a hawthorn hedge a fine herd of cattle grazed among buttercups on sunlit grass. Jerry remembered the thin and often diseased cattle he had been accustomed to see years ago on the common. Surveying the boundary he realised that these healthy beasts were his grandfather's property and as far as he could tell all the previous common was now Ridgeway land.

He noticed a high, thick beech hedge growing on a steep bank. He recalled it vividly from childhood but decided not to put Columbine to it. It might strain the mare. Very few horses could attempt it but he remembered that his father used to clear it easily on a massive roan eighteen hands high named Black Devil which had been as famed for its bad temper as for its strength. But Jeremiah Ridgeway had been proud of the animal. Some of his notoriety had been gained through his exploits on Black Devil. The thought came unbidden into Jerry's mind that his father must have done something reprehensible about which he had never been told. Surely his grandfather wouldn't loathe his son's memory so much merely for the wild pranks in which Jeremiah habitually indulged. There must have been something more. But here Jerry stopped his own thoughts. It was disloyal to think such a thing of a man who had been the sort of father many a boy would have loved to have, sharing Jerry's childish amusements until the day a bolting team overturned a phaeton, killing both Jerry's parents. It was typical of Jeremiah that he had been attempting to drive two very unsteady horses in tandem and only because someone had bet him that he couldn't do so.

It must be the sight of old territory which had caused these morbid musings, thought Jerry. He wasn't normally such a fool. Best to concentrate on something else such as who was the pretty little housemaid who didn't appear strong enough to scrub the floor?

3

CLARE was in Jerry's room because cleaning the bedchambers was part of her job. She gave a most unnecessary polish with beeswax to the clothes press. Mallow, Jerry's valet, was bending over the ponyskin trunk and unpacking the captain's clothes.

Mr Ridgeway entered the room in a dark red dressing-gown and leaning on his stick. He struck this on the floor sharply twice to attract attention. Clare jumped but Mallow merely turned slowly round and looked the old gentleman up and down with deliberation. "Do you want something, sir?" he asked in a tone of voice which implied that Mr Ridgeway had no right to cross the threshold of Jerry's room.

"My grandson. Where is he?"

"The captain has gone for a ride, sir."

"When will he be back?"

"I cannot tell you, sir. I do not ask the

captain what he is going to do; I take my orders from him."

There was a moment's silence. Clare held her breath, afraid that one of Mr Ridgeway's famous outbursts of temper was about to explode. It might have done but something caught his eye which interested him.

Mallow was lifting a mahogany box on to the table. With his handkerchief he delicately wiped away a thumbmark from the brass plate on the lid. The old gentleman moved nearer.

"What's that?"

There was a slight hesitation. Mallow was averse to Mr Ridgeway's manner but he was really very willing to show the contents of the box. He opened the lid slowly and spoke in a calm but impressive voice.

"It is the sword presented to Captain Ridgeway by the underwriters and merchants of Lloyd's to mark his gallantry in battle. His conduct at Trafalgar was extremely brave but it was particularly remarkable in so young a captain."

Almost reverently Mallow lifted out the sword while Mr Ridgeway leaned forward and noticed the ivory grip and gilt knuckle-guard. Mallow slowly withdrew the blade from the black leather scabbard whilst Clare completely forgot her menial status and came forward to examine it, too. Mr Ridgeway did not notice her, his gaze was riveted on the damascened steel blade with a design picked out in gold.

"Hold it still a moment," he commanded. "I want to read it." His eyes travelled up from the crown and GR, past the figure of Victory and a sea monster with a lion's head to the simple inscription recalling gallantry in action at Trafalgar and the name: Captain J. Ridgeway.

For a second Clare didn't see the sword. Instead she was haunted by two laughing black eyes as she had been during the night. Then she turned and looked at Mr Ridgeway.

He was oblivious of her. His eyes were moist, he swallowed hard twice and a muscle twitched in his cheek. Then in a voice which was intended to be brusque but in fact was husky he said, "Yes, very well. Put it away safely."

And he went out of the room, blowing

his nose vigorously.

Mallow did not vouchsafe another word and Clare returned to her cleaning. She had only been in this house for two months but it seemed like a peaceful retreat in contrast to her previous place of work. After the deaths of her parents she had been obliged to take work as a housemaid in the first position available.

Her father had been a gardener when he married in clandestine circumstances the daughter of his employer. He had taken his bride, Isabella, to London and succeeded in establishing himself as a market gardener. A friend, he said, had provided the finance necessary for him to set up his nursery in the fields near Chelsea but over the years his lack of business acumen had been serious in its effects. He paid for the production of beautiful books of botanical drawings, for he proved to be a skilled artist, and he even propagated some new hybrid plants but he did not make money. Until her death Isabella lived in blissful ignorance of their pecuniary difficulties. But when Thomas Winster followed his wife to a premature grave,

Clare discovered a disastrous number of debts. She was grateful for the assistance of a neighbouring lawyer and determined that every penny should be paid.

There was no house or land to sell; they were rented. She relinquished them and sold all her parents' effects. She was particularly regretful at parting with her father's books and paintings but they were her only lucrative asset. The solicitor was remorseless in assessing the financial value of each item and, after the lawyer's fees had been deducted, she was given the balance — a mere two pounds.

So with that small sum, her own clothes and her mother's workbox, which she had quietly retained as her sole tangible link with her former life, she answered an advertisement for a housemaid in the London home of Lord and Lady Corton.

Her ladyship relegated her maids to a dormitory in the attic storey. Clare was unpopular with the others who slept there because she disturbed their rest with almost continuous coughing for six weeks during the winter. The room was cold and the walls showed patches of damp — a striking contrast to the sophistication and comfort of the rooms where Lord and Lady Corton lived and entertained their guests. In many of these chambers the walls were covered in coloured damask whereas on the top floor the naked plaster showed dark smudges of moisture. Clare was fastidious enough to wash her whole body every day even though the only water available to her was stone cold. In the winter she sometimes had to break the ice off it. Undoubtedly these conditions contributed along with some very foggy days to cause the persistent cough which made her so unpopular with the other maids. She understood how necessary sleep was in a job which started long before daylight. Her own experience of rising in the pre-dawn cold of a garret made her sympathetic towards them. She was embarrassed by a cough she could not control.

Friendless among her colleagues, she was also the target of the housekeeper's ill-temper. One day when she was supposed to be cleaning the stairs she was discovered leaning over the banister to support herself, racked by a paroxysm of coughing and gasping for breath.

The housekeeper's voice could be heard all over the building. "You were told to clean those stairs. Why aren't you doing so? Answer me that. Why?"

Clare thought the reason was obvious but, anyway, she couldn't speak.

It was on those same stairs that her employment in the household was finally terminated.

Normally she was expected to use the backstairs and remain out of the sight of her employers. On this occasion she had been sent to clean a room which opened off the half-landing. She was just outside the door when Lord Corton started to climb the bottom flight. Clare was standing under a Venetian window through which the sunlight illuminated her hair, emphasising the red lights in it and accentuating her pale skin. Food for the servants in this house was meagre and illness had deprived her of her appetite throughout the winter. Consequently she was thin and pallid but her delicate features remained attractive and as she curtsied demurely she was unaware of the effect her appearance might have.

As she lowered her eyes respectfully the baron noticed the way her dark lashes curled against her white cheeks. He was a middle-aged man whose excessive predilection for food and drink had made him so corpulent that even the waistcoat, received a month ago from his tailor, was already strained across his stomach. Ascending the stairs had already made him breathe heavily but he had plenty of energy in his rotund body.

"Come here, my dear!" he ordered and gave her no chance of disobeying. He simply seized her round her slender waist in a swooping movement which was observed by another housemaid on the upper landing.

Polly, a heavy girl with thick legs and fat cheeks, was renowned for her sulkiness. She had achieved a certain status by her ability to imitate Clare's refined voice in an exaggerated manner, which caused much mirth. She sneaked off to report to her ladyship, who happened to be a few yards away, that Clare was not working properly. Lady Corton had forgotten who Clare was but she peered over the banister and bristled with indignation.

Lord Corton was obviously inebriated and held Clare against him in a grip which hurt. He fastened his hot, damp mouth on hers, smothering her face until she could not breathe. She was actually glad when his wife's crisp, contralto voice called down to the half-landing. The peer suddenly released Clare and she fell against the wall, banging her head so hard that she had a tender lump on it for days.

Lady Corton dismissed her at once and Clare went out into the streets with all her belongings in one carpet-bag.

She stayed overnight in a dismal inn and read in the newspaper the next day an advertisement for a housemaid at Ridgeway Manor in Dunnock Green — her mother's native village. Feeling alone in the world, she thought it might be comforting to be near her mother's home. Mrs Panton, recognising the name, was eager to have her. Mr Ridgeway accepted her into the household, saying, "I suppose I'd better. If it wasn't for Jeremiah you probably wouldn't have been born." Clare didn't know what he meant.

When her mother had married Thomas Winster, her family had ceased to acknowledge her. It was unlikely that they even knew of Clare's existence. Isabella had written a few letters home to her father, Titus Crewe, but they had been returned unopened. Clare knew she bore a strong resemblance to her mother, although her green eyes and the red glints in her hair were distinctive. Isabella had not had those, so perhaps Mr Crewe would not recognise Clare. Clare had no intention of approaching a grandfather who refused to acknowledge her mother.

Now, as she rubbed the window pane thoroughly, she could see the fence where Mr Crewe's land met that of the Ridgeways. She looked at it for a few moments and then applied herself to washing the window-sill.

By the time Jerry strolled along to the library the old gentleman's mood had changed. Half an hour spent dwelling on the significance of that presentation sword had been succeeded by an hour's irritation with the young man who had kept him waiting.

He lay back in his chair, with his striped waistcoat strained across his stomach, and snorted as his grandson entered the room.

"When I was a young man," said Mr Ridgeway surveying Jerry's breeches and riding-boots, "I wouldn't have gone into my grandfather's presence splashed in mud."

"No, I'm sure you wouldn't," agreed Jerry amiably. "Your grandfather died before you were born."

Mr Ridgeway frowned which caused his bushy eyebrows to meet above his nose and gave him the appearance of a bird of prey. This belied his real feelings. Secretly he was rather amused at Jerry's retort. "Old Culpepper was as fit as a fiddle a month ago. He's dead now. It'll be my turn next, so you'd better learn to manage the estate."

"Nonsense! You're a long way from your grave and would be further if you didn't imbibe so much port!"

"Scoundrel!" retorted his grandfather but there was no anger or malice in his voice. He moved over to the mahogany knee-hole desk, drew out the chair and sat down heavily on it. He spread out the map of his lands while Jerry came and stood beside him, a hand on the back of the chair, and leant over the map.

"Crewe and I don't mix socially." Mr Ridgeway spoke brusquely as though he didn't want to be asked for details about his relationship with his nearest land-owning neighbour. "But we managed the enclosure between us."

His hand, its dry skin taut and blotched with brown patches of pigment, moved across the map. "Out here we've got wheat."

"Part of the old north field, eh? Have you done anything about drainage?"

"Why?"

"From what I can remember, old Fletcher's strips used to be like a swamp after heavy rain. They were somewhere around here, I think."

"Yes, that's right." Mr Ridgeway had no intention of telling Jerry that he was pleased with his analysis but he did inform him in detail of the measures taken to drain the land.

Then he heard hooves on the gravel and glanced out of the window. "There's that damned fellow, Bromley. His father was a cit. I don't know why he must needs come calling here. You can give me a glass of that sherry. Tell Hedges to deny me if Bromley wants to see me."

He was too late. As Jerry passed him a delicately engraved wineglass the door opened.

"Mr Bromley and Master Roger Bromley,"

"Hell and the devil!" swore Mr Ridgeway, spilling sherry from a shaking hand.

"Which is hell and which is the devil?" asked Jerry *sotto voce*.

An appreciative gleam lit Mr Ridgeway's black eyes.

Mr Bromley, a red-faced man with bushy side-whiskers, wore a blue coat over his rotund stomach. Not waiting for the old gentleman to speak, he extended his hand saying loudly, "Good-day to ye, sir."

"Hmph!" vouchsafed Mr Ridgeway.

Mr Bromley was not discomposed.

"And how are you today, Squire?" he asked.

"Riddled with rheumatism and very busy," growled Mr Ridgeway, looking ostentatiously at the clock on the mantelpiece.

"Sorry to hear it! Sorry to hear it! Warm weather brought on the twinges, eh?"

"They're not just twinges!" snapped Mr Ridgeway, rising easily from his chair. "It's a wonder I'm not bent double with the pain in my back."

"Pretty bad, is it? Roger, give Mr Ridgeway his stick and help him to the sofa."

The youngster, who had bright blue eyes and a snub nose, advanced reluctantly. Jerry winked at him, received a mischievous smile in response, and listened with amusement to his grandfather. "I'm not in my dotage. I don't need to lean on anyone. But if you've brought the boy he may as well be useful. Get me the footstool from behind that screen, Richard."

The lad obeyed and Mr Bromley reminded his host that his son was called Roger. Mr Ridgeway ignored this, lowered himself into the wing-chair and discovered that he had left his sherry on the desk. He gestured towards the boy with his stick. "You! What's-your-name? Rupert. Fetch my glass. Now, Bromley, what have you come for?"

"We have come to see the hero," beamed Mr Bromley.

"Come to see who?" snapped Mr Ridgeway.

"Anyone who has helped to trounce Boney is a hero, sir," declared Mr Bromley.

Mr Ridgeway was mollified. He indicated Jerry with a sweep of his hand and said proudly, "My grandson, Captain Ridgeway."

Jerry advanced with a friendly smile and outstretched hand.

"And who's this?" he asked, turning to the boy whose shy grin and adoring eyes were fixed on him.

"Eh?" Mr Ridgeway looked up. "Oh, that's Richard."

"I'm Roger."

Jerry poured a glass of sherry and handed it to Mr Bromley. Mr Ridgeway frowned; the trouble about offering drinks to visitors was that they stayed longer.

"You've already caused a stir in the village, Captain. Everyone's remarking on your impressive appearance astride that spirited mare of the squire's. Got as good a seat on a horse as your father, I'm told."

"What do you know about my son?" demanded Mr Ridgeway, his eyes inquisitorial beneath their grey brows.

"Almost nothing," admitted Mr Bromley and saw his host give a sigh of relief. He turned to Jerry. "I have been hoping to get to know you, for I have followed your gallant exploits ever since I first heard of you."

Mr Ridgeway raised his head, his heavy brows knitted together in a puzzled frown. "You knew about my grandson, sir?"

"Of course. I have a brother living near Portsmouth. He has sent me the relevant copies of his newspaper."

Mr Ridgeway longed to know more; at the same time he didn't want to reveal how little notice he had taken of his grandson over the past fourteen years.

He said as casually as he could, "Wrote a nice piece about him, did they? On what occasion was that?"

"At the time when Boney was building a fleet of flat-bottomed boats to invade our country. The newspaper recorded Captain Ridgeway's daring attacks on the little ports. He towed away a barge from one under cover of darkness."

"Mentioned that, did they?" asked Mr Ridgeway and wished he had known about it himself.

Jerry said nothing but he grinned reminiscently and played with Horatio's ears.

"I remember," continued Mr Bromley "that when he was later given a man-of-war, great play was made of the name of his ship and your grandson was called the Audacious Captain."

"Was that your nickname in the navy, Jerry?" asked Mr Ridgeway.

"No, sir. They called me Ribald Ridgeway."

Mr Bromley laughed — a rumbling guffaw, but he rubbed his hands together with satisfaction. He said, "I understand that a large crowd assembled to cheer you last time you embarked upon the *Audax*."

"They flattered me." Jerry was embarrassed and went to pour himself some more sherry.

"Sir, will you tell me about the battles you won?" pleaded Roger.

Jerry laughed. "I didn't win 'em single-handed, you know."

He produced a fine model of a 74-gun frigate delicately carved from bone which he had purchased from a French prisoner of war. This diverted the lad's attention from personal questions and Jerry adroitly turned the conversation with Mr Bromley to the prospects for the coming harvest, but Mr Ridgeway's mind was pleasantly occupied.

He would have Jerry's portrait painted, depicting him in dress uniform with his hand resting on the hilt of his sword. Perhaps the *Audax* might appear in the background. Who was the best artist to execute such a portrait? Expense didn't matter. Head and shoulders alone would not be enough; it must be a full-length portrait.

The old man was quite surprised when

Mr Bromley got up to go, and after he had gone he remarked, "Bromley is pretentious and smells of the shop but he is not without intelligence."

"He struck me as a well-meaning fellow."

"Anyone can be well-meaning," said Mr Ridgeway dampeningly.

Jerry hoped the visitor, who was still in the hall, couldn't hear this.

He couldn't. Hedges was just handing him his hat, while Clare, who happened to be walking out of the dining room with a jar of beeswax in her hand, curtseyed modestly. Mr Bromley had been about to step outside but he turned and looked at her again.

She did not appear like any ordinary housemaid. There was no embarrassed giggle at being seen in the front of the house by a visitor. She lowered her head respectfully as she made her polite obeisance but her movements were dignified and she did not appear to demean herself.

She reminded him of someone.

He remarked about the weather to Hedges and tidied the frilled collar which

Roger wore outside his nankeen jacket. These manoeuvres were a pretext for remaining in the hall until the girl had passed through it. He was watching her the whole time.

"Who is the new housemaid?" he asked.

"That is Clare Winster, sir."

The elegant carriage of her head, the arched eyebrows, the straight nose and the well-formed mouth. He'd seen them all before.

Hedges, who shared Mr Ridgeway's opinion of the genial gentleman, politely but firmly ushered him down the steps.

Suddenly, just as Roger, ensconced on his grey pony, was protesting that he did not need a leading rein, Mr Bromley remembered where he had seen those features.

He decided that in the course of the next few days he would pay a visit to Crewe Hall.

4

TRUE to his word Jerry did not wear lace ruffles when he dined with his grandfather that evening but he was attired in a speckless black coat which fitted exactly across his shoulders and his neckcloth was well starched and intricately tied. Mr Ridgeway viewed him with silent pleasure. He even raised his quizzing-glass to take a second look.

Jerry recognised the convex lens in its elegant gold frame with a handle which he had often seen in childhood. That spy-glass had been his father's. Oddly enough, Mr Ridgeway had retained one of his son's possessions when he had thrown out all the rest. "I don't want anything that belonged to him in here," he had pronounced bitterly when the orphaned Jerry had arrived with two servants and two carriages full of baggage. Most of the items had never been unpacked. The whole lot had been burnt.

"Jerry, you're not listening!"

"What? Oh, no, I wasn't," admitted Jerry with a disarming smile. "I'm not a good listener. It's much easier to be the talker, you know!"

"Well, my boy, perhaps you're right."

Mr Ridgeway sat at the head of the table but he left the carving to Jerry, who noted with amusement that a very good wine stood on the sideboard beside which Hedges was hovering respectfully.

Mrs Scorby normally gave Clare an extra plateful of the food left from Mr Ridgeway's table. When Clare first arrived in Dunnock Green, Mrs Scorby had been horrified to see her sunken cheeks and craggy elbows. If you accidentally touched the girl you could feel her ribs. "What you want is plenty of victuals," said the cook firmly and commenced from that day to supply Clare every evening with a plateful of 'extras' which the old gentleman had ignored. The incredible thing was that Clare didn't put on more weight.

She didn't eat the additional food. She would ask to be allowed to take it upstairs to have later. If she encouraged mice into her bedroom Mrs Panton would be vexed. But perhaps she couldn't consume so much all at once after being so used to not having enough to eat. So Mrs Scorby acquiesced and Clare frequently took a small bundle out of the kitchen — spare food wrapped in a napkin.

But she didn't eat it.

When she had a free hour she would walk in the countryside because she loved the fresh air after the dark basement and grim attics of the London house.

It was on one of her rambles that she first met Fred and Maggie Colt. Dispossessed of their cottage by the enclosure, they lived as squatters in a secluded piece of woodland on Mr Ridgeway's estate. Maggie was not old but she looked as though she was. Exposed to the damp and cold she had developed a bronchial cough. Clare remembered vividly her own long bouts of weakness and coughing. She recognised Maggie's need for nourishing food but the Colts made her promise not to tell anyone where they lived, so she couldn't ask for food to give them but neither could she buy it.

All the extra food which Mrs Scorby

gave her, Clare secreted away until her next opportunity to take it to the squatters.

"I can't understand it," said Mrs Scorby anxiously. "I do what I can but Clare don't get no fatter."

"It's not your fault, Annie," said Mrs Panton. "Some people are skinny by nature." But privately she was worried.

Mrs Scorby was, however, delighted by the reception given to her culinary skills on the second evening of Jerry's return to Dunnock Green. She was very glad to see empty dishes returned to the kitchen. Hedges conveyed a message from the captain, complimenting her on an excellent repast. Even Mr Ridgeway had enjoyed his food.

Mrs Scorby sat down on a chair by the kitchen fire and fanned herself with a pudding cloth.

"I'm real pleased," she declared. "Didn't I say Master Jeremy would like that beefsteak?"

Everyone dutifully agreed and Mrs Scorby declared that what she herself wanted was a 'nice cup of tea'. She gave Clare a key and told her to unlock the caddy and fetch some. She quite forgot to give the thin kitchen maid any 'extras'.

When Clare reached her tiny bedroom late that night her mind was preoccupied with the Colts. She had planned to slip out and take them some food in the morning. The long summer days dawned so early that she knew she would waken at four, but she didn't have to begin work until half past five. That would be long enough to enable her to take a parcel of food to them.

But she hadn't got any tonight and it was several days since she had been to them. Maggie would be getting weaker.

Long after everyone else had gone to bed Clare was standing at the small mildewed mirror on her chest-of-drawers. She whipped off her cap and brushed her hair; then she made a decision.

She put down the hairbrush and opened her door cautiously. She listened tensely. No sound except for Mr Hedges snoring. Holding her rushlight in one hand and lifting her skirts gingerly with the other, she negotiated the stairs and slid silently into the kitchen quarters.

It was difficult to see with only the

rushlight. In the darkness she collided with the corner of the dresser and bruised her thigh.

After that she walked carefully through the shadows, avoiding the flitch of bacon which had been hanging for three weeks. Clare reached the stone shelves of the larder.

The hashed calves' head had been eaten and the roast duck with green peas was finished. Mr Ridgeway had consumed more than his usual amount while discussing with Jerry the drilling of seeds, the usefulness of turnips for winter fodder and the appalling behaviour of the French army in Spain. Jerry himself had eaten a considerable quantity of beefsteak and followed it with a strawberry cream.

Even so, Clare found part of a pigeon pie, some cold lamb and half an apple tart. She took the three dishes to the kitchen table, where she had put a white cloth. As quietly as she could she began to remove the pigeon pie from its dish.

If Mr Ridgeway had heard noises after dark he would have sent for Hedges and ordered him to pursue the intruder with a poker. But it was not Mr Ridgeway who, alerted by a creaking board, had listened to the stealthy opening of the kitchen door and now heard Clare drop the spoon.

"Who's there?" The question was rapped out in the abrasive manner of one upbraiding a lazy seaman.

Clare jumped, terrified, and opened her mouth to scream but no sound came as she turned to face the light of an oil-lamp in the doorway.

Captain Ridgeway was pointing a gun at her.

She couldn't move. She just stood there, rigid with fright and crimson with guilt.

He was attired in loose-fitting, blue brocade dressing-gown fastened round the waist with a cord. But all Clare could notice was the lamplight glinting on the silver-mounted duelling-pistol levelled at her.

"What a fool I am! I thought I should find a housebreaker." Jerry calmly placed the pistol on the table and surveyed the food.

"Hungry? Let's have something to eat then."

"No, no! I couldn't eat anything."

Of all the people in the world to have caught her apparently thieving! Colour flooded her face. When this episode was over she would try to persuade herself that she did not care for his opinion of her, but she did — dreadfully.

He said, "Your hair's very pretty. I like it without the cap. Do you have to wear one during working-hours?"

She nodded miserably. His manners were aimed at avoiding unpleasantness and putting people at their ease; that was why he was paying her compliments. She was sure he didn't mean them; he was sorry for her — a thief caught in the act.

She tossed her hair back in the manner of a nervous pony and so revealed her thin shoulder. He touched her lightly in a gesture meant to reassure her and was appalled to feel her shoulderblade almost cutting through the thin material of her working gown.

"You ought to eat that food, you know."

She shook her head unable to speak for the lump in her throat. No doubt he thought she stole because she was so desperately hungry. It was kind of him to say she could have the food.

"It's not for me."

"Isn't it?" His voice was gentle but disbelieving. "Who is it for then?"

"I can't tell you."

"Do you mean that my grandfather has servants who are not properly fed?"

"No. It's not for anyone in this house. I can't tell you more."

"I see."

But he didn't; she knew that. She looked at the modest assortment of viands on the small white cloth. She wouldn't be able to take them to the Colts now. And Maggie needed food.

A tear trickled down her cheek. She brushed it away impatiently with the back of her hand.

"You'd better have this." He pulled a clean lawn handkerchief from his pocket.

"Thank you. Shall I be dismissed?"

"What for?"

She gestured towards the food.

"Because of that! How can I dismiss you for that? I can't count how many times I stole downstairs and had a feast in here when I was a boy. Rabbit pie, cold ham, plum cake. Anything I could find. I thought I was so clever, too. Looking back on it I believe Mrs Scorby left them for me. I'll wager she knew all the time. Of course, my grandfather didn't. He'd have licked me hard but I thought it was worth risking that. I still think you ought to be eating this. Shall we both have some now?"

"No, thank you." There was an infinitesimal sob in her voice. He was being very kind but everything he said proved that he believed her to be taking the food for herself.

And she couldn't tell him the truth. She hadn't to reveal the secret of Fred and Maggie Colt.

She gathered up the food and replaced it in the larder. Returning to the kitchen, she curtsied and said with quiet dignity, "I'm sorry I disturbed your rest, Captain Ridgeway. May I go to bed now? Goodnight, sir."

"Goodnight Clare."

He watched her walk out of the room, her narrow shoulders bowed, her hand shielding the simple rushlight. He stood with compressed lips surveying her.

She looked very vulnerable.

"Can you manage with that thing? Why don't you take this?"

She winced at the word 'take' but turned back to see him offering her a pewter candlestick with a new candle in it.

So it wasn't a sarcastic remark. He was being kind again.

"Thank you, sir." She took it, curtsied once more and withdrew.

Jerry stood beside his oil-lamp with a frown on his forehead, then picked up his pistol and dropped it in the pocket of his dark blue dressing-gown.

★ ★ ★

It wasn't often that Mr Bromley had any contact with the owner of Crewe Hall and he had never paid a morning call on him previously but he prided himself on having the nose of a bloodhound for scenting out mysteries. He was certain that he was on the track of one now and he meant to 'sniff it out', as he told his wife. To succeed in this he would have to endure the penetrating and cold gaze of Titus Crewe, but he considered it worth while.

He went past the lodge and down the main avenue to Crewe Hall. He passed the pond — one might almost call it a lake — where a pair of ornamental ducks swam between the water-lily leaves. The white stone of the little temple gleamed against the azure sky. A spade, a rake and a watering-can nearby showed that it was really a sophisticated toolshed.

Mr Bromley was escorted to the library by Harper, who looked as though he would rather not undertake the task. He opened the door, announced the visitor and withdrew smoothly.

Mr Crewe made no attempt to rise from his desk or take a chair near the fireplace. He made a weary gesture towards a seat and Mr Bromley lifted his coat-tails and sat down. This position on the other side of the large desk made it appear as though he was being interviewed.

"What is your business?" asked Mr Crewe.

"I — I came to make a morning call."

"Really? How kind of you!" The even tones were quite expressionless.

"It's a — er — a social visit. I thought it was time I paid a courtesy call on you."

"I see. I do hold a Public Day every summer in July."

Mr Bromley perspired heavily and wiped his brow with a large handkerchief. Titus Crewe observed this with a very slight frown, as though he had seen a dog scratching in the drawing-room.

Mr Bromley's discomfort increased under the scrutiny of this man with pale green eyes. He clasped his hands between his knees and rubbed them together in a nervous gesture and then realised that this movement was also being observed with a mixture of disgust and tolerance.

In the silence which followed, the ticking of a gilded French clock sounded unnaturally loud. A portrait of an early seventeenth-century Crewe, in armour and just managing to control his mettlesome horse, took up the whole length of the west wall. A large tapestry depicting the amorous lives of the Greek deities hung above a Boulle cabinet.

"Nice place you've got here," ventured Mr Bromley.

Titus Crewe inclined his head and George Bromley winced at the sound of his own voice, feeling as he had done on Sunday when he knocked over a pile of prayer books during the sermon. He glanced towards a silver tray containing an assortment of crystal decanters and wished he could have a drink. Titus Crewe saw the longing look and ignored it. People like Bromley became garrulous if given good wine and he did not think this manufacturer could have anything to say worth hearing. Very few people had.

Mr Bromley crossed and uncrossed his leg awkwardly and caught the polished desk with the toe of his boot. Titus Crewe said nothing but he looked at the boot.

Then he took a gold watch out of his pocket and placed it on his desk, then began tidily to sharpen a quill-pen. His visitor became afraid that if he didn't find some conversational gambit his host (if he could be called that) might actually start writing. Well, if he had to talk he might as well broach the subject he had come to discuss.

"Very fine painting on the stairs."

"There are six canvases hanging on the staircase wall."

"The one of the girl."

Mr Crewe laid down the penknife. "It is by Romney," he said in even tones.

"Your daughter I presume, sir?"

"Yes."

"Fred Colt told me about her. Isabella, I think you called her?"

"That is so. I am afraid I have no idea who Fred Colt is."

At last they were beginning to talk. Mr Bromley undid his coat button and eased himself back in his chair. "Fred Colt used to have a cottage on the old common."

"Did he? I never remember the names of any of the villagers."

Mr Bromley took out his handkerchief again, shook out its folds and applied it once more to his forehead. "Very hot day, isn't it?"

"You appear to find it so."

Mr Bromley avoided Titus Crewe's eyes, which were unemotional and yet daggerlike in the intensity with which they could search another man's face. He looked instead at the silver pen tray engraved with the Crewe arms and continued his comments on the Romney portrait. "Beautiful girl. Lovely features, good figure and that fair skin. I've seen the picture once before — when you sent for the Turnpike Trustees. I've not forgotten the picture. Charming. That's how I came to recognise your granddaughter."

Mr Crewe fixed his penetrating gaze on Mr Bromley. "And where do you suppose that you have seen a granddaughter of mine?"

"At Ridgeway Manor. She's a housemaid there."

"Hardly!" Mr Crewe's lip curled sarcastically.

"Her features are just the same as those of your Isabella, but she's got some red in her hair and her eyes are green — like yours." He was about to add 'only warmer', but he decided not to.

"The fact that Ridgeway is employing a pretty maid who resembles Isabella does not mean that the girl is her daughter. I am said to resemble the Duke of

Cumberland, but that does not make me His Royal Highness's son."

"You never know!" said Mr Bromley in a jocular attempt to relieve the atmosphere.

Mr Crewe's face did not alter but he said very quietly, "I expect you wish you had not made that remark, Bromley, so I won't comment upon it."

Mr Bromley flushed crimson. A fly entered through the open window and he was just about to swat it as he would have done at home when he realised that this was not the place to swat flies.

Mr Crewe glanced distastefully at the insect and said, "I'm sure you will excuse me, Bromley, if I attend to my work. I have a letter to write to the Parliamentary Commissioners."

"That's all right. I'll be going."

"Harper will show you out." Mr Crewe rang a bell which was immediately answered.

George Bromley got up and was about to stretch out his hand to shake that of Titus Crewe but the latter was already writing. He looked up briefly to say, "Harper, when you have escorted Mr

Bromley out, return here. I wish to speak to you."

"Yes, sir."

The door closed behind the unwelcome visitor and Titus Crewe put down his pen and stared unseeingly at the tapestry. Could it possibly be true? And if so, what was Ridgeway's motive in employing her? There was only one answer: If the girl was Isabella's daughter, then Jeremiah Ridgeway was adding further humiliation to the Crewes.

Probably she was not Isabella's daughter. Bromley had put two and two together and made five.

But had Ridgeway intended people to do just that?

The door opened and the butler appeared.

"Harper! I feel that a man in your position should have enough sense of responsibility to know when to deny his employer. It ought to have been obvious to you that I didn't wish to speak with that person."

"I beg your pardon, sir. He said he fancied you would wish to see him."

"Then he was over-fanciful. But you

do not take your orders from casual callers. It is I who employ you and I shall not continue to do so if you make that error of judgment a second time."

"I beg your pardon, sir."

"That is all right. Everyone makes mistakes sometimes." But the tone implied that Mr Crewe really meant 'everyone except me'.

5

JERRY was listening to the song of a great tit and thinking that there were many compensations for not being at sea; when his path emerged through a tangle of thick bushes to a small clearing where the ground was springy and covered in moss. He stood still abruptly with an exclamation of surprise.

In the space was a wooden hut with a rather crudely thatched roof and a window without any glass. A pig rooted among the undergrowth and smoke twirled through the opening in the roof which served as a chimney.

A man of about fifty-five in a homespun smock emerged from the shack and looked warily about him.

"What the hell are you doing here?" exclaimed Jerry while Horatio's ears flattened for a moment against the back of his head.

Then the dog bounded forward with the white tail wagging. He jumped up putting his forepaws on the man's smock.

"Down, Horatio!"

"It's all right, sir. He's a nice dog and I wouldn't 'urt 'im."

"Fred Colt!" Jerry strode forward, hand outstretched. "Whatever are you doing here?"

The man looked at the proffered hand as if unsure whether or not he was meant to take it. Then he rubbed his own grimy one down the smock and grasped Jerry's.

"Beg pardon, sir. I didn't think anyone'd find me 'ere, wot with old Mr Ridgeway being stuck indoors like. I did 'ear 'e wasn't likely to last long."

Jerry laughed. "That was just some maggot he's got in his head because his rheumatism's plaguing him. But it's too bad for him to walk this far, certainly. So, you're hiding from him, are you? Why?"

"I can't find nowhere else to go, sir."

"But surely you had a cottage on the common?"

"Yes, sir; but since t'common's been enclosed I 'aven't got nowhere."

"But they must have given you some other land!"

"No, sir. I 'adn't got no proof that I'd lived in t'village long enough."

"But you've lived here ever since I was born. Surely that was explained to the commissioners?"

Fred sniffed and regarded Jerry through watery blue eyes. "Bill Brown spoke up for me but 'e lost 'is cottage and I reckon other folks were a bit too nervous to say anything like."

"Nervous of what?"

"Well, sir, the commissioners were very respectful to Mr Crewe and to your grandad."

Jerry ground his teeth. "The hell they were! You'd have thought the commissioners, who were supposed to divide the land impartially, would have had more backbone than to give in to a couple of greedy old men." He regarded the hovel frowningly.

"Per'aps you'd condescend to step inside, Mas — " Fred corrected himself quickly. He had been about to say "Master Jeremy" to the man he had taught to climb trees when he was a little boy. "Mebbe you'll come in, Captain, sir. Maggie would love to see ye but she's bad with 'er chest these days."

"Is she? That's because she's exposed to the winds and rain in this place."

Jerry had to bend his head and shoulders when he entered the low doorway. Inside, a middle-aged woman, who seemed prematurely old, was ladling potato broth into two pewter bowls. She was seized with a violent fit of coughing, so she didn't immediately raise her head but when the paroxysm ceased she wiped her eyes and became aware of a shadow falling over her.

"Master Jeremy! It is, isn't it?"

"Yes, Maggie. "

"I wouldn't 'ave believed it! You 'ere!" Then her smile vanished. "Master Jeremy, you 'aven't come to turn us out, 'ave you?"

Since there was no spare chair, he dropped onto one knee on the beaten earth and took her hands in his. "Do you think I would?"

"No, no, Master Jeremy, I don't but your grandad might force you to — only

I don't suppose 'e knows we're 'ere. You see, what happened was — " but further coughing nearly made her choke.

"Don't try to talk; I know. Fred's told me. First of all, stop worrying about my grandfather. He is not going to evict you."

"Are you sure, sir?" asked Fred eagerly.

"Quite sure."

"You mean you won't tell 'im about us?"

"I shall certainly tell him."

Fred shook his head. "Then he will turn us out. I could mebbe get a job in one of them manufactory towns, but I doubt Maggie could stand it."

"Of course she couldn't. Stop being so frightened of my grandfather, Fred. If I say he won't evict you, he won't. You'd better gather together your possessions, borrow a handcart and trundle them down to the cottage Abel Harrison lived in. It's still empty since he died, although I dare say it's in need of cleaning and repair. Then you can come round to the home farm for work on Monday. There'll be haymaking, hoeing and God knows what else to do."

"You could do with me temporary-like?"

"No, permanently."

"But if your grandad finds out where we're living 'e'll be that mad 'e'll kill us."

"He won't trouble you at all. I'll see to that," said Jerry with a grim note in his voice.

They tried to thank him but he only chuckled softly and said, "Do you remember the day you made me a rabbit pie, Maggie, after Fred and I had been fishing?"

"Aye. I remember but I dare say your grandad didn't like you to be so late 'ome."

"He nearly had the hide off me!" Jerry laughed.

Maggie put a third bowl of potato broth on the table and said emphatically, "It's a good thing you've come 'ome, Master Jeremy."

It didn't seem to occur to either of them that he wasn't going to stay. Jerry pulled an upturned barrel to the rickety table, picked up a piece of bread and with perfect equanimity broke it and dunked a piece of it in his soup like his hosts did, while he reflected that perhaps he was going to have to stay. He already knew Jenkins was to be given command of the *Audax* and he himself was to be offered a first-rate, the *Cleopatra*. If he refused it, he would be unlikely to receive employment again. Then he looked up at the spare faces beside him. If you had got to renounce something you wanted, it was better to accept the fact than fight against it.

Maggie suffered another bad bout of coughing but when it was over she looked at her husband and said, "Fred, just think of it! Master Jeremy back 'ome and drinking my pertater soup! If I'd known last winter when I were laid up with that inflammation of the lungs that Master Jeremy was coming back, I'd 'ave known I was going to get better." She gasped for breath and then looked at the captain. "To tell you the truth, sir, I didn't think I'd live through the winter, but you see summer's come again and you're back. It just shows, don't it?"

Jerry nodded and tried to swallow

another mouthful of potato soup. God! what a tasteless liquid it was! No doubt they could win the war without him but someone had to feed these people.

"Is Clare all right? We 'aven't seen 'er for a few days," said Maggie.

Jerry looked at her intently. "Clare?"

"Your grandad's 'ousemaid."

"Sh! Maggie!" besought Fred. "You didn't oughter say nothing about Clare."

"Why not? Master Jeremy won't be angry with her just 'cos she brings us food from the manor. She said it was all leftovers and Annie Scorby told 'er she could 'ave it."

"Aye, but Annie don't know she brings it 'ere."

Jerry suddenly felt very lighthearted, coupled with a strong desire to see Clare again. "I think she's well but she seems rather thin."

"'Er mother was always a slim lass."

"Her mother?" Jerry wanted to know more but the arrival of Horatio triumphantly bearing a rabbit interrupted the conversation and, without waiting for an answer to his query, he exclaimed, "There's your dinner, Maggie. Well done,

93

Horatio! For a dog that's been reared at sea you're a credit to me. It proves that one can adapt to anything." He added the last remark to himself.

He did not revert to the subject of Clare because Fred, overjoyed at Jerry's return and the prospect of earning a living, became quite vociferous.

"Do you remember," he asked "when you climbed the church tower to settle a bet about 'ow many birds' nests were in the belfry and you rang the bells? We all thought t'French 'ad landed."

"I remember it well." Jerry laughed. He didn't explain that the panic which ensued so infuriated his grandfather as to cause that final painful interview when Mr Ridgeway evicted him from the manor (declaring "You're getting too much like your damned father,") and Jerry decided to go to sea.

He left the Colts, feeling unusually pensive. The sun percolated through the leaves. Horatio pushed his nose among the downy seedheads of dandelions. The wind lifted the branches and ruffled the leaves and the constant motion produced a continuous hushing sound.

Jerry stopped, sat on a fallen log, pulled a long blade of grass and chewed it thoughtfully. Before long he would be compelled to get in touch with the Admiralty . . .

He sighed, then got up and walked with resolution towards the manor house.

There appeared to be considerable poverty among the villagers; perhaps his grandfather might listen to reason but he remembered that his father had referred to Crewe as 'a merciless devil'. Jerry himself would have called Titus Crewe 'a cold fish'. God alone knew what would happen if those two selfish old men hatched any more plots to enrich themselves. He had to stay.

The sky was very blue — made him recall that day in the West Indies when he'd caught a French ship off the coast of a sugar island. That had been one of the *Rainbow*'s most successful encounters. It didn't do to think of it now but she was a lovely frigate, the *Rainbow*.

He suddenly turned to the left, strode into the stableyard and called for Columbine to be saddled. Ten minutes later he was galloping like a demon across the turf. His short hair was ruffled and the mare's mane and tail streamed out behind her. Mile followed mile until he reined in, thoroughly exhilarated, and surveyed the fertile plain and, in the misty distance, the line of hills marked by a white horse of prehistoric origin. This was his land and he was part of it and he wasn't blue-devilled any more. He had something he wanted to tell Clare.

He wheeled his mount round and rode for home.

Clare had just finished cleaning the dining-room. She looked up at the portrait of Jeremiah Ridgeway now hanging where that of Colonel James Ridgeway used to be. She regarded the square brow of Jeremiah Ridgeway beneath the lightly powdered hair. He, too, had the same long nose, thin lips and determined chin which were characteristics of his father and son. His eyes were the same black and they 'crinkled' at the corners like Jerry's did but they were not quite so merry. She could have fancied there was a hint of something else in them as well — hard to define but haunting.

"Whatever people say about you, I like

you. I feel as if I knew you somehow," she thought.

The voice of Hedges broke through her reverie. "Clare."

"Yes, Mr Hedges."

"Captain Ridgeway wants to see you now in the morning room."

"Now?"

"Yes. You'd better go at once."

Her mouth went dry and she felt sick. He must have changed his mind. He was going to dismiss her after all because she had taken food from the larder. Of course, Mr Ridgeway was really her employer but if the captain decided to dismiss a servant she was sure his grandfather would acquiesce.

She wished she could have had longer to prepare herself for the coming ordeal but it was only a short passage which separated the dining-room from the morning room. She was soon there. But she was fighting against a sense of humiliation as she knocked softly on the door.

"Come in!" The captain's voice was always penetrating. To her apprehensive senses it now sounded like a pistol shot.

She entered quietly and closed the door behind her, hoping no one would hear what he said to her, although when she was dismissed they would probably discover the cause. The morning room was a small parlour prettily furnished in the style fashionable during the Eighties of the previous century when Mr Ridgeway's wife had purchased the dainty furniture. Neither her husband nor her grandson normally made use of the room, but Clare had recently polished the brass fender and dusted the chairs, which were upholstered in rose-patterned brocade. Although it wasn't a large room, it appeared big to Clare now.

Moving with innate dignity she seemed to glide across the carpet. Captain Ridgeway was standing at the far end of the room. He suddenly seemed a very overpowering figure in his brown cloth coat, riding-breeches and top boots. It appeared a very long way across the room towards him and the approach was worsened by the unnerving sight of the captain tapping his boot with his riding-whip. It was an idle gesture of which he was unconscious but to Clare it seemed menacing. She was aware of having to make a positive effort to walk up to him. Her legs felt stiff and unwilling to move.

His shoulders were broad and he was very tall. She had never felt so small as she did now.

At any moment that quarterdeck voice would blurt out a tirade against her.

"Well, Green Eyes?" The tone was gentle and half teasing.

She relaxed slightly and curtsied demurely, her long skirts swaying from her slender waist.

"I want to thank you, because I think you've been looking after some old friends of mine — Fred and Maggie Colt."

Relief flooded over her, but this was no moment to think of herself. She said seriously, "They need help."

"Yes, I know, and they're going to get it. He'll soon be employed on the manor and we've a cottage they can have."

"Oh, thank you!" she exclaimed involuntarily and added hesitantly, "I apologise for taking food from Mr Ridgeway's table but until last night it was always given to me for myself, so I felt I was only giving my own supper away. I didn't look upon it as wrong."

"It shouldn't have been necessary for you to use subterfuge. They ought to have been provided for. You're not to blame, but I'm very angry that they've been destitute. Anyway, they'll be moving into Hawthorn Cottage. It's by the boundary of the old east field."

"Yes, I know it. I'll help them to move but they will need to borrow a barrow from here. Is that all right?"

"Of course. They'd better have a handcart but you can't push it."

"Maggie isn't able to help Fred."

"What about my grandfather's gardener?"

"No; his corns are too bad. He's been to Mother Wiggins for one of her remedies, so I'm afraid they'll get worse." The green eyes were alight with merriment now.

Jerry retorted, "He always walked like a flat-footed duck when I was a boy. I'd lay any odds there are numerous bottles under his bed. He's got gout, mark my words!"

They laughed in perfect rapport until he

said, "Why did you look so apprehensive when you came into the room?"

"I was afraid that you had decided to dismiss me after all."

"I'd no idea I was such an ogre. It's probably my damned voice. It's more suited to shouting above the noise of the wind in the canvas. Let me make one thing clear: If I thought you had to take food from the larder to appease your hunger, my anger wouldn't be directed against you but towards those who should have seen that you had enough to eat."

"Thank you."

His voice was unusually quiet as he asked. "Why didn't you tell me about the Colts? Didn't you trust me?"

"I promised them I wouldn't tell anyone and I couldn't break my word."

"Of course not."

"I did wish I could tell you, though." The green eyes were frank and somewhat wistful.

He took a step forward and then drew back. She was a servant in his grandfather's house and she had no one to protect her from him. His caresses might not be welcome and she had no power to prevent them. He restrained himself and wished she wasn't so cursed pretty.

Clare asked, "Mr Ridgeway will consent to them living on the estate?"

"My grandfather will do what I say!" he decreed. Then he gave a half-apologetic laugh. "That sounds egotistical, doesn't it? Of course, I shall have to let him win some arguments — it's only diplomatic — but definitely not this one."

"Thank you. I will ask Jack to help me move them, then."

He had a sudden revulsion against seventeen year-old Jack with the red cheeks and bovine intellect assisting this dainty creature in any way. "We'll move the Colts tomorrow and I'll come to help."

"But it's not a suitable job for you."

"My dear girl, when you've spent hours in a bloody and smelly cockpit after a battle, there's no job left that's not suitable!"

He wasted no time before striding into the library.

Mr Ridgeway was reading *The Times*. He put it down and remarked, "I wondered where you were, but Hedges said you were talking to Clare."

"I was."

"I intended to mention her. She's no ordinary housemaid."

"That's obvious."

"Yes, well, I thought I'd better tell you in case you think of seducing her."

"In case I what?"

"Seduce her. She's very pretty and you're young and healthy and living under the same roof."

"I may be young and healthy but I do not seduce housemaids."

"Don't you?"

"No! You've got a mind like a muddy pool."

Mr Ridgeway chuckled and waited for Jerry to ask more about Clare's background. He would have done so except for the urgency of settling the problem of Fred and Maggie.

Mr Ridgeway looked up questioningly. "Well?"

"I think we must understand one another, sir. When you sent for me I believed that you were ill and wanted a companion for a short time. That was

103

not the case. Your health is tolerable and what you are really asking is that I should settle here permanently to assist you in the management of your estate. Until two hours ago I was not prepared to do that. I have changed my mind. Provided that I am allowed to redress the evils which attended upon the enclosure, I will stay and help with your land."

A pulse throbbed in Mr Ridgeway's temple. "And just what do you mean by 'the evils' of the enclosure?"

Jerry poured himself a restorative glass of wine and sat down opposite his grandfather. He had no intention of prevaricating. "I have just discovered the Colts."

"Ah good." The old gentleman sighed with apparent relief. "That little grey by Hanover out of Victorious is like to make a good hunter."

"I am not referring to horses." Jerry set down his glass on a piecrust table and stared at his grandfather in an implacable fashion. "If you don't know who I mean you ought to do."

"And if you don't know how to speak respectfully, it's time you learned."

"I have to feel respect in order to speak respectfully."

An alarming colour suffused Mr Ridgeway's face. "I didn't send for you to order me around in my own home."

Jerry ignored the purport of this and concentrated upon one phrase. "Have you ever considered what it would be like if you didn't have a home?"

"No why should I?"

"Because that is the situation to which you have reduced Fred and Maggie Colt."

"Who are they?" Mr Ridgeway's brows met in one of his intimidating frowns.

It didn't unnerve Jerry. "They inhabited a cottage on the common."

"Oh! That pair of squatters. I always thought it was a diseased pig of Colt's which caused fever among the swine some years back."

"Fred and Maggie were rendered homeless by the enclosure. They are subsisting on the scantiest diet in a rough shack in the woods. If they continue there through another winter I believe Maggie will die."

"Yes, I should think she probably will. You didn't think to offer me a glass of that Madeira you poured for yourself."

Jerry lost his self-control. Picking up his own wineglass, he hurled it into the fireplace, where the crystal shattered into fragments.

Something almost like a chuckle escaped the old man. "So you've got the Ridgeway temper, have you? I thought you always laughed at everything."

"I don't laugh when people are made destitute by my grandfather's avarice."

Mr Ridgeway opened and shut his mouth several times but seemed unable to form the words which would have described his feelings adequately.

Jerry regained his composure first. He got up and went to the side-table, where he poured two glasses, one of which he handed silently to his outraged relation. Mr Ridgeway swallowed some hastily but his colour was increasing to a choleric puce. "I think you'd better explain yourself," he said shortly.

"Perhaps I had. Fred Colt possessed a meagre cottage on the common when I was born. He certainly lived in it for the regulation twenty years before enclosure took place. Therefore he should have been given adequate compensation for it. Instead, he has been evicted and left to fend for himself. He and his wife are now living in a makeshift shelter and are actually afraid that you will turn them out of that."

"Where are they?"

"In Brock Wood."

"No wonder they're afraid. They're trespassing."

"They won't be trespassing much longer." Jerry started to speak in what he himself, called his 'poop-deck voice'. "I have just taken Fred on as an extra hand permanently and they will be moving into the cottage Harrison used to have."

"Don't think I shall abdicate my authority," stormed Mr Ridgeway. "This is my house and my land."

"It is, sir; but if you wish me to administer it I shall have to do it in the way I believe to be right. If you don't want me to use my own methods you must get an agent who will obey you in every detail."

"Scoundrel!" The old man banged the

floor with his stick. "Impudent young whipper-snapper! How are you to learn to run the place if you don't get any practice, eh? Of course I shan't get an agent. You'll do it yourself, damn you!"

Jerry bowed ironically. "Thank you, sir. In that case the Colts will have Harrison's cottage and you will employ Fred."

With these words he walked out of the room ignoring his grandfather's comments about ungrateful young men who deserved to be horse-whipped.

Jerry went into the hall. Near the stairs he encountered Clare and grabbed her arm.

"Clare!"

"Sir?"

"The old man's a dreadful colour. I'm responsible for that, I'm afraid. Can you soothe him?"

"I think so. If he gets very upset I usually have a game of chess with him."

"No doubt that's part of your duties as a housemaid!"

She dimpled responsively.

He said, "It's my fault. I suppose

I should have been more tactful but I was so furious about the treatment of the Colts. But he looks as though he'll have an apoplexy and, to tell you the truth, I'm quite fond of the old bas — " He corrected himself hastily, his eyes twinkling again. "Of the old gentleman."

She laughed. "Don't worry. He'll be all right again once he concentrates upon his game. Besides, he'll be able to tell me how badly I play and that comforts him a lot."

"Bless you!" He patted her slender shoulder and she forgot to curtsy or call him 'sir'.

Her prognostications proved correct. By the time Jerry returned to the room an hour and a half later Mr Ridgeway's colour was normal and he was criticising his opponent. "You were so busy defending your bishop that you threw away your queen."

"Yes. That was very foolish of me."

"Never mind. You do your best. Is that you, Jeremy? Come and look at this board. I'll show you how I achieved checkmate. Half an hour ago the positions were something like this." He began replacing men on the chequered board.

Jerry winked at Clare but he gave patient attention to his grandfather's recollections of his own strategy. "This is where she made her worst mistake. See? She moved her white bishop there and exposed her queen. That was a reckless move and enabled me to win much sooner than I should otherwise have done."

Clare got up and looked at the fireplace where broken pieces of crystal still glittered in the candlelight. Jerry made a wry grimace and said, "I'm afraid I lost my temper."

"It ought to be cleared up," said Clare.

Mr Ridgeway raised his head from the contemplation of the chessboard. "Yes, it ought. Well, don't just stand there, girl!"

"No, don't; do sit down, Clare," said Jerry with a sparkle in his eyes as he pulled out a chair for her.

She shook her head. "I'll get a brush and sweep it up."

"You'd better not. If he tells you to

sit down, you'd do well to obey," said Mr Ridgeway querulously. "That's what we shall all have to do. I dare say he'll be wanting me to uncover my head and say, 'Aye, aye, sir,' before long."

Jerry laughed. "No; but if you throw the Colts out of that cottage, I'll clap you in irons!"

Mr Ridgeway smiled a little but he suddenly looked tired and announced that he was going to bed. He added with an almost pathetic note in his voice, "You will stay, Jerry?"

"Yes, I'll stay but I shall do things my own way, mind."

"Very well. Ring for Jack. He can support me upstairs."

"He hasn't my stamina. You'd better lean on my arm, sir."

"Aye." The old man nodded and added with deliberate ambiguity, "I shall have to lean on you."

6

CLARE sat up suddenly. She ached all over from weariness but that had to be ignored.

She had promised the Colts that she would clean Hawthorn Cottage this morning. Maggie certainly hadn't the strength to do so and she didn't think Fred could make a very good job of it.

She tied an apron over her gown and ran downstairs to splash her face with cold water and collect brushes and rags and bucket. Mrs Panton had said she might borrow them and she had promised to work later that night to make up for the fact that she would be starting later this morning. She turned the large iron key and let herself out of doors to walk down the lane.

A hare bolted in a straight line down the path ahead. In a blue sky, frothy white clouds rode high.

She reached Hawthorn Cottage, where fragrant red roses climbed up the mellow brick wall and honeysuckle rambled over the fence, perfuming the little garden.

There was no doubt that Hawthorn Cottage needed cleaning. Fortunately, it only had two rooms, the upper one reached by a ladder. She suspected that some wild animal had found a refuge there for a while and that the village boys had played games in it. Luckily, its period of vacancy had been short but Clare found that the scrubbing took longer than she expected. Once she trod in something soft and squelchy. She screamed and discovered it was only a rotten apple.

By the time the job was finished the sun was much higher in the sky and she was covered in dust. She couldn't let Captain Ridgeway see her like this.

She set off for the house, running frantically with the bucket banging against her leg. Her breath came in gasps and she got a stitch in her side.

She arrived hot and exhausted in the kitchen. Mrs Scorby exclaimed in horror. "You'll kill yourself, Clare Winster, trying to clean up for a feckless couple who'll make everything as bad in a few days.

You've no sense but you've a kind 'eart. Betsy, you'd better fill a bath with water."

"Oh, thank you!" gasped Clare.

She bathed and washed her hair before putting on a clean gown. It had better not be her maid's uniform. She hadn't to ruin that. This necessitated getting out one of her own gowns. She put it on and brushed her hair. No need to wear a cap.

She hurried down the drive and found Jerry leaning against the wall of the lodge.

"You didn't wait for me? Sir, I'm sorry."

"You were worth waiting for."

Her hair had dried but remained very soft and the wind blew tendrils around her face. The gown, although worn and faded, was of a pale green shade which complimented her hair. The sun burnished its auburn lights and now that it was flowing freely over her shoulders Jerry discovered that it was much longer than he had realised.

Under his appreciative scrutiny the embarrassed flush flooded her cheeks and added to her discomfiture. But this ceased when he began to recount hilarious stories of the idiosyncrasies of the pressed men on board the *Audax*. They walked down the road past the turnpike and into the village, where they had agreed to meet Fred.

"Show us where everything is, Fred. We mustn't waste time," said Jerry. "You'll need to clean the place before night-time."

"No, sir. Clare's been and done it, 'aven't you, lass?"

"First thing this morning."

Jerry swung round to face her. "One of the village women could have done it or that kitchen maid, what's-her-name? You ought not to have done it."

"The Colts are friends of mine." She watched Jerry lift a heavy box and added mischievously, "One of the men from the village could do that."

He grinned at her. "The Colts are friends of mine."

Fred, himself, was leaning on a spade. He was out of breath and it occurred to them both that he looked exhausted.

"Why the spade, Fred?"

"It's this way, sir. I may need the tools wot belonged to me dad. I 'ad 'em in a big box like and I buried them under t'bush near the Red Lion."

"Give me the spade and show me where the buried treasure is." Jerry held out his hand, took the implement and strode off to the inn.

Fred confidently indicated a currant bush and stated that his father's box was underground on the right of it.

Jerry dug energetically for some time but uncovered nothing. He wiped his brow. "Fred, are you sure you planted it as deep as this?"

Fred rubbed his nose thoughtfully in a gesture Jerry remembered from childhood. "You know, Captain, sir, I reckon I've made a mistake. It were by t'second bush on third row but counting from t'other end."

Jerry looked into the deep pit he had dug and doubled up with laughter, then shouldered his spade and walked along the edge of the currant bushes beside the orchard fence. He put the spade in and, placing his foot firmly on it, commenced to dig. He tossed aside piles of soil and

116

Clare murmured, "Fred, you are sure it was here, aren't you?"

"Quite sure, lass," he answered readily. "At least," he added as Jerry's excavation grew apace "I think it was."

Clare longed to laugh but she was afraid that the captain, who was hot and dishevelled, might be angry. She pressed her lips tightly together to prevent them from twitching and stared down at her toes.

A voice beside her said, "You may laugh."

She looked up into the merry black eyes and gave way to her mirth.

"Fred," said Jerry, "Are you really certain this time? Because if you're not I shall soon have dug up all Joe Bates's kitchen garden."

Fred grinned and assured him that he really was certain.

Jerry dug rapidly, his spade struck something hard and to Clare's relief Fred ejaculated, "There! That's me dad's tool box like I said."

Jerry hauled it out and handed it over. Colt began to dust the box by rubbing it up and down his trouser-leg. He wanted to open it at once and show them each of the tools individually and explain what his father had made with them but Jerry entered a caveat. "It's time we loaded up the cart, Fred. Where's Maggie?"

"I've took 'er to Hawthorn Cottage already."

They repaired to the stables. Jerry washed his hands and arms up to the elbows under the pump and quenched his thirst with ale. Then he trundled the cart towards Brock Wood to collect the couple's scanty belongings. Fred gave some of them to Clare to carry in a box.

There was a horse blanket, which he had been given by a friend of his who had been a groom at Mr Crewe's stables. "See there — in the corner — T.C. Them's Mr Crewe's initials."

"It was very kind of Mr Crewe," said Clare innocently.

"Oh, 'e didn't know nowt about it," said Fred frankly. "''E mebbe wouldn't 'ave liked me to 'ave it."

Clare opened her mouth in a gasp, caught Jerry's eye and sat down suddenly, helpless with giggles.

"You're a good lass but you do waste time," complained Fred.

She got to her feet and walked beside the two men. Her arms ached as she tried to carry her pile of goods. The pain shot up into her shoulders and her face became paler than ever. Jerry suddenly noticed and insisted that she ride. "Come on, we'll push you."

He stopped the cart and lifted her to sit on a heap of objects, adjuring her to hold tightly. They proceeded along the dusty lane where the smaller wild flowers were hidden by tall grasses near the ditch.

Fred was eager to hear about Jerry's experiences in the navy and although the captain was always reticent to talk about his successes, he had a repertoire of funny experiences to relate. He came to the end of an account of the peg-legged cook in the galley who had an unfortunate encounter with a pig in the manger. The pig, which had been intended to provide pork for Jerry's table, proved to be a character and eventually the captain gave instructions that it was on no account to be killed. It was finally entered on the ship's books as Able Seaman Hogg and became quite a pet.

"Didn't nothing ever go wrong?" asked Fred.

"Now and again," said Jerry lightly. "This country doesn't spend much money on its ships. When I had command of the *Rainbow* she was so rotten that we had nothing but a sheet of copper between us and a watery grave. It wasn't the best time to fall in with a couple of enemy frigates." He laughed. "We beat 'em off but it looked hazardous for a while. That was when poor old Peters was killed and we had a damned great hole blown in the bow."

"You must have been in danger of sinking!" Fred removed his misshapen hat and scratched his head.

"It did look like it, but I took soundings and found that if we did go to the bottom the flag would still be flying."

"You've not changed, lad," said Fred.

The captain changed the subject. He began to tell them about a Turkish pilot he had taken on board to guide him up the Tagus when he was to disembark troops at Lisbon. He stopped to wipe the sweat from his brow and gave a hilarious imitation of the pilot. Clare, sitting on the pile of 'odds and ends', laughed until the muscles of her waist ached.

None of them saw the figure watching them.

Mr Crewe had ridden down to the eastern boundary of his land and, although he was hardly visible behind a thick and straggly hawthorn hedge, he had an excellent view of the little procession.

Fred and Jerry were pushing the cart together. Atop a pile of oddments, which included a battered cauldron, the table and barrels and a straw pallet, sat Clare leaning back with her hair flowing around her shoulders and her face lively with laughter.

"Isabella!"

Titus Crewe gave an audible gasp and the hands which held his reins began to shake.

The girl looked so like her. It was just as though he was seeing Isabella again. How often he had criticised her for a lack of seriousness and tried to restrain her from contact with the lower classes.

121

This was Isabella's daughter. There could be no doubt of that.

And presumably that young man with the hearty laugh was Captain Ridgeway. He looked too much like Jeremiah, damn him!

Why ever was he pushing a handcart filled with useless rubbish? There were enough men employed at the manor to undertake all menial tasks, so why should he put his weight behind the primitive vehicle?

They passed the thick hedge where Titus Crewe literally shook as he sat astride the powerful grey. Jerry made some jocular remark and elicited a musical laugh from Isabella's daughter.

It was like looking back into the past. Titus Crewe took one more look at the sunlight on his granddaughter's hair. Then he wheeled his horse about and galloped away.

When he re-entered his house his servants recoiled from the expression in those ice-green eyes hooded by heavy lids. He spoke more quietly than ever and that was a sign of his anger. It was not enough for the Ridgeways that Jeremiah had ruined his hopes, now Jeremiah's father and son would humiliate him further.

But not if he could avoid it.

He sat down at his desk and drew a sheet of paper towards him while Fred Colt's simple belongings were trundled through the village.

There was the scent of newly mown hay which Jerry hadn't smelt for years. The grass, which bordered the lane, was spattered with the bright yellow of dandelions. A wood-pigeon cooed from the beech tree and a magpie flew above the cottage gardens where the delicate colours of columbine grew beside the brilliant orange of marigold.

Perched on the cart Clare had a good view over garden walls. Her lofty eminence also gave her a new perspective over the churchyard. The cart made only slow progress past it and she had time to gaze over the ivy-covered wall and even to decipher the writing on a plain tombstone near the lych-gate. It simply said: Jeremiah Ridgeway 1761 – 1790.

It said nothing about his character,

unlike the plaque on the north wall of the chancel which depicted an urn with funereal drapings and recorded for posterity in grandiloquent terms the many virtues of Lucius Ridgeway who 'departed this life in the year of Our Lord one thousand seven hundred and fifty-six, mourned by his family and lamented by his friends and the many recipients of his beneficent generosity!' For Andrew Ridgeway there was an alabaster memorial in the form of a classical sarcophagus which almost filled the south transept, seriously impeding the progress of anyone who tried to walk that way. But for Jerry's father there was only this simple, upright, weathered slab of grey stone. Why?

Fred's goods were conveyed without further incident to Hawthorn Cottage, where Jerry lifted Clare down from the cart before he began to unload it.

When the captain removed his watch from the pocket of his breeches, Clare glanced at the time. "I must run down the field path. Mrs Panton will be wanting me."

Jerry grabbed her wrist as she was

about to leave. "No; you will come with me. No field paths for you, my girl. You might meet the village idiot."

"That's right," agreed Maggie. "Poor Daft 'Arry goes that way sometimes. I did 'ear your grandad wanted him to be confined as a dangerous lunatic but Mr Bromley says 'e ain't as bad as that. Just simple like."

Clare found herself propelled to the door and led towards the village. Flame-coloured poppies swayed in the breeze, ivy clustered round the bole of an oak tree and cows grazed among a profusion of buttercups. Two cock pheasants were in combat, their jewel-coloured feathers shimmering in the sunlight. The path rounded a corner and emerged beside the wall of the manor garden.

Clare entered the house by a servants' entrance, Horatio chased the stable cat and Jerry went into the harness room to speak to his grandfather's head groom.

Mr Ridgeway surprised his household by the sudden increase in his activity during the next day or two. He sent for Cavalier, a solid, strong roan capable of carrying any weight, and rode round his estate with Jerry. He stopped at intervals and gestured with his riding-whip towards improvements.

"What do you think of that, eh?" he would ask and Jerry told him honestly. Jerry's knowledge of recent agricultural improvements coupled with his vivid recollections of the land around Dunnock Green enabled him to make perceptive comments.

When they approached a thick hedge on a bank with a ditch in front of it, Mr Ridgeway said, "I hope you're not going to jump that. Your father once broke his collar-bone trying it."

Jerry said nothing. He opened the gate for his grandfather to pass through, then shut it, rode back a short distance and thundered up towards the formidable obstacle. Watching to see that Columbine was ready with the correct leg, he touched her haunches lightly with his whip at precisely the right moment and cleared the barrier easily, landing with his mount under perfect control.

He rode up to his grandfather who said, "You're a fool but, thank God, you've got spirit."

The villagers looked with admiration when they saw the Ridgeways riding together down the lane. The old man with his white hair and heavy eyebrows was still a handsome, commanding figure. His grandson, who rode with such easy expertise and raised his hat to every woman — even old Nell working the village pump — had the same air of authority.

When they returned, Mr Ridgeway was tired, swore at Jack, hurled abuse at Hedges and went upstairs to rest on his bed with the red brocade curtains drawn round it. Later Jerry went to visit him.

Mr Ridgeway greeted his grandson with a string of swear words ending in the accusation, "Hedges tells me he can't bring me any more port because you've ordered him not to do so."

"That's right," said Jerry cheerfully.

"How dare you?"

"Easily. The doctor says you've been having far too much of it. You're a wicked old devil but I've no desire to attend your funeral for many years yet so you'll drink less port. It's no use blaming

Hedges either, because he's only obeying my commands."

"You're an insolent young puppy!" snapped Mr Ridgeway.

"Yes, aren't I?" agreed Jerry.

"And what are you plotting? I can see by your face you're planning something."

"Only a village cricket team."

"Bah!"

Jerry sat near his grandfather and added, "I think we should hire one of the best rams to improve our flock, sir. It's worth twenty guineas to have a really prize specimen for a season."

"Twenty guineas of my money, you mean."

Jerry smiled. "It will be a very profitable investment and well you know it. If you're doubtful, just study these weights and prices. I have the latest list from Smithfield."

"All right. I'll look. No doubt you'll get your own way."

Jerry grinned. "It seems a long time since I was in this room."

"Probably the last time was when you crept up and put a hedgehog in my bed — a damned, flea-ridden creature and I dare say you've not forgotten what I did about it."

"No. I still get twinges. Most people think the wound was caused by a French musket at Trafalgar."

"Scoundrel!" said his grandfather in a voice that failed to be ferocious. "Take yourself away and leave me in peace. I don't want to see you again until I eat my mutton."

"The pleasure is mine!" retorted Jerry.

His grandfather threw his stick at him with surprising force and accuracy. Jerry put up his right arm and caught it in mid-air. "Pity you're too old to be in my cricket team," he remarked before he went out of the room whistling.

★ ★ ★

Mr Crewe's butler met Hedges sometimes in the butler's pantry at Ridgeway Manor, where Hedges generously offered Harper a glass of Mr Ridgeway's port.

On one such occasion Hedges had indicated the bruise on his temple caused when Mr Ridgeway threw a boot at him. Harper had informed him that physical attack was nothing. It was far worse to be confronted by the frigid stare of Mr Crewe.

"Since the captain came home things have been a lot better at the manor," Hedges said. "Mr Ridgeway actually thanked me for something the other day and Master Jeremy often makes him laugh. It'd do Mr Crewe good to laugh."

"I doubt it," said Harper pessimistically. "He hardly ever smiles but when he does he looks as though he's satisfied with some scheme he's worked out and you wonder who'll suffer for it."

After the visit of Mr Bromley, Titus Crewe became even more quiet and remote, so everyone at Crewe Hall moved softly. The sight of Mr Crewe coming along a corridor at some distance from his private apartments so terrified a small maid that she burst into tears. It was therefore no surprise when Harper was summoned to the library and told to get rid of her.

"I can hardly be expected to employ such a lachrymose female."

"I'm sorry, sir. Her father died recently

and she has twin brothers who — "

Mr Crewe raised his hand a few inches. "I don't think I have time to listen to the unfortunate young woman's difficulties, Harper. It is a pity she cannot forget them when she is in this house at work. But if she is in trouble I suggest you inform the Overseer of the Poor."

"Yes, sir."

"And, Harper . . . "

"Yes, sir." The butler was apprehensive. He hadn't forgotten the threat of dismissal which he had received after allowing Mr Bromley into the presence of his employer. Harper had a widowed mother who depended on the sums of money he was able to send her.

"I believe you are acquainted with Hedges, Mr Ridgeway's butler. Perhaps Hedges has mentioned to you that there is a housemaid at the manor named Clare Winster. I believe her to be a relation of a man who was once in my employment. I should like to be assured that she is well treated. Does Hedges ever refer to her? Has he, perhaps, informed you of the terms on which she stands with her employer?"

Harper hoped his friend would forgive him for a breach of confidence. "He did say that Mr Ridgeway treats her in an avuncular manner."

"Indeed?" The cold green eyes met those of the uncomfortable butler. "And has Hedges given you any indication of how Captain Ridgeway treats Clare?"

"I understand the captain behaves in a very friendly way towards her."

"Like a brother?"

"I suppose you could say that."

"Is it what Hedges said?"

"Not exactly, sir."

"What did Hedges say?"

Harper clenched his hands and felt the palms damp with perspiration but he did not dare lie to this man whom one could not deceive. "Hedges said that Captain Ridgeway looks at her in a way that's a bit more than a brother, if you know what I mean."

"Thank you, Harper. What you have told me is most interesting and helpful. You may go."

The door closed gently behind the butler.

Mr Crewe looked for a few minutes

through the window towards the little Doric temple where the gardeners kept their tools. Then in a decisive gesture he selected a quill and sharpened it with a penknife.

He covered a sheet of expensive paper with his neat regular handwriting, folded the letter tidily into three and melted some wax, dropping the red blob on to the paper and impressing it with the seal which he wore set in a gold ring. It depicted a snake strangling a stoat, the design deeply incised into a piece of amber.

He addressed the letter to Miss Winster and rang the bell. A footman was to deliver it to the servants' quarters at Ridgeway Manor and there was no need to wait for a reply.

7

CLARE was in the garden and did not see the messenger arrive.

The sun was so bright that when she stepped indoors everything appeared dark green by contrast. She carried a basket filled with fragrant rose petals for Mrs Panton to make pot-pourri. She looked at the flesh-coloured petals of the cuisse de nymphe roses mingled with dark crimson petals. In the garden a thrush trilled melodiously and bees hummed among the stalks of lavender.

The kitchen smelt of newly baked bread. Mrs Scorby gave her some which was dripping with butter from the home farm.

Jack came in. "Letter for you, Clare."

Mrs Panton leaned forward. "Clare, if you want to go into my room to read that you can."

"Thank you."

Clare went quietly to the housekeeper's room and sat down at the gate-legged table beside a framed picture of a ship drawn rather inexpertly by Jerry at the age of eight.

She broke the seal and opened the double page. Seeing the words 'Crewe Hall' in the top right-hand corner she dared to hope that perhaps her grandfather wanted to meet her.

Dear Clare,

Naturally, I have your welfare at heart and therefore I hope that you will accept my advice which is given with the intention of saving you from the acute embarrassment that will inevitably come to you otherwise.

Mr Ridgeway probably admitted you to his establishment out of benevolence. I have a feeling that he wished to atone for one of the more grievous of his late son's many wayward acts. I understand that Mr Ridgeway treats you with a degree of consideration unusual towards a servant. Of more concern to me is the knowledge that his grandson has been seen to behave towards you as though you were his equal. In the eyes of society this must brand him either as one who is not naturally capable of living up to his status or more probably as one who flaunts his mistress in public.

Consider the embarrassment which the captain must suffer when he marries, as he inevitably will, an attractive young woman and brings her home to find a pretty maid in her establishment who is receiving preferential treatment. I think she would ask his grandfather to dismiss you. The most dignified course for you to take is to leave now, unobtrusively and without explanation. I suggest the latter course because I am sure that if you explained your true reasons to your employers they would feel their only honourable course would be to persuade you to stay. However, it would not be in their interests for you to remain, so I trust that your innate unselfishness will prevent you from mentioning the matter to them.

You could leave at night on the mail coach which changes horses at the Red Lion at three in the morning.

I assume that you will be able to

obtain a reference from your previous employer, but if this should prove impossible write to me. I should be happy to provide you with a testimonial, so that you may seek a suitable situation in the capital.

Yours etc.,

T. Crewe

Clare felt hollow and weak. She realised that Mr Crewe wanted her to leave Dunnock Green because he did not wish to be embarrassed by the child of his daughter's marriage to a gardener.

Nevertheless, she feared that what he said about the trouble she could cause the Ridgeways was true.

It had never occurred to her previously that she had presumed upon Mr Ridgeway. Still more worrying was the reference to his grandson.

At times the captain had behaved as if he'd forgotten that she was an employee and she blushed as she recalled that once or twice she had forgotten that herself. Recently, when she was sitting on the cart, she had actually teased him. He had laughed, but, of course, that must have been because he was too kind to snub her.

She had never thought of Jeremy Ridgeway marrying, but now that he was home again his grandfather would be invited to take him to dine in many houses where there would be some lovely young ladies as dinner partners for him.

Yes, people would be horrified if they thought the captain had a close relationship with a maid in his home.

She was disappointed because Titus Crewe was her only relation and he had rejected her.

When she rejoined the others for their meal in the servants' hall every mouthful seemed dull and dry; and it was difficult to swallow.

Betsy counted plum stones and recited, "Tinker, tailor," until she reached the end of the rhyme. "Thief! Ugh! I don't want to marry a thief. Can I 'ave some more? Clare, you've only ate four. That's not much. Tinker, tailor, soldier, sailor. You've got sailor, Clare. Which sailor are you going to marry?"

Clare's face flushed and Mrs Panton said sharply, "If you've got nothing better to do than recite silly rhymes, Betsy Miller, you can go and scrub the kitchen floor."

Betsy looked mulish and muttered something about people 'picking' on her.

Because Clare knew she had to leave them so soon, the sights and sounds and smells of Ridgeway Manor seemed all the more attractive that evening. There was the silver bowl full of red roses on the hall table, the chink of balls as Mr Ridgeway and the captain played billiards together and the perfume of lavender wafting through an open window.

She overheard Mr Ridgeway say, "We'll accept that invitation from the Norbys and I shouldn't be surprised if Crewe invites us to dine now that you've come home."

"The last time I tasted any of his food it was sour apples."

"Sour apples? Oh, yes, I remember. You used to climb the trees and rob his orchard. Why the devil did you do it if the apples were sour?"

"That was your fault," retorted Jerry cheerfully. "You gave him permission to thrash me for it, so, naturally, I continued to steal them. You shouldn't have done that, you ought to have beaten me yourself."

"I only said he could thrash you IF he caught you."

"He never did!"

"I knew he wouldn't."

They both laughed.

Clare had no desire to eavesdrop, so she hurried away but she had heard enough to be convinced of the relevance of her grandfather's warnings. She had to go before she could cause difficulty for Captain Ridgeway; in fact before he began to mix with local society. And that meant immediately.

Tomorrow she had to slip out unobtrusively before the outer doors were locked and go to the Red Lion, where she hoped to be allowed to await the arrival of the mail coach. Had she enough money for her seat? She thought so.

She worked late, then crept into bed so tired she could hardly see, and dreamt that she was lost.

8

THE following morning Clare packed her few possessions into a carpet-bag. She felt regret at leaving the housekeeper who had treated her so kindly. She had never worked so hard in her life as she did that day. She not only did everything Mrs Panton asked of her but also cleaned all the door furniture until she could see clear reflections in the knobs and keyhole covers; she even shook out Horatio's bed and brushed him so that he wouldn't shed hairs on the newly cleaned carpets. She had done two or three days' work in one.

As the hours wore on the threat of rain increased until by early evening they were menaced by a dark grey sky tinged with yellow.

"I'm glad to see you're back, sir," said Mrs Panton when Jerry walked into the hall. "There'll be a terrible downpour soon and you would have got soaked."

He laughed. "It wouldn't have been a new experience."

"Well, I dare say you did get spray on the deck," she said.

He shook his head in silent amusement. Poor Panny! How horrified she would have been if she had seen him dressed in his foul-weather clothing on a poop-deck awash with water while his ship was tossed about like a cork on the ocean. No other officer was near him. Only his superior physical strength and his faith kept him from being swept overboard.

He went upstairs chuckling and Mrs Panton stood looking after him with a puzzled expression on her face. This gave Clare her opportunity. She propped a letter of thanks and farewell on the table in the housekeeper's room, pulled her cloak over her shoulders and slipped out of doors.

As she went down the path the first heavy drops fell, to leave coin-sized spots on the flagstones. Clare left the path, skirted the back of the lavender bed and climbed the stile which gave access to the meadow.

The heavy cloud, which had caused

the headaches of which both Mrs Panton and Mrs Scorby had complained, began to discharge in rain over the field path. Clare pulled the hood of her brown cloak over her coppery hair. The rain fell more and more quickly, and yet she was so tired that she hardly noticed it.

But when the rain became a deluge, it was impossible to ignore it any longer. She would be soaked soon and she was so weary it was difficult to keep walking. If she stopped to shelter she didn't think she would be able to begin walking again. She remembered that there was a shorter route to the Red Lion if one went slightly to the west, along the rutted lane which traversed the edge of the old common, now Mr Ridgeway's barley field.

This was the vicinity which Daft Harry frequented. She recalled that neither Maggie nor Captain Ridgeway had wanted her to wander alone along these paths. However, not even Daft Harry would be likely to venture out in such a downpour. She wondered where he lived, but soon forgot him as the long shafts of rain stung her face and the heavy droplets bounded high off the path in front of her. The hot sunny days which had preceded this weather had baked hard ruts in the path where the farm wagons and carts had dug trenches. Now the rain ran down these gullies.

Resolutely she continued westwards. She hadn't to remain under the same roof as the Ridgeways. The captain's future in society depended upon her leaving. She could not let him down.

The hems of Clare's skirts grew damp, her foot slipped and she nearly fell. Twisting herself quickly, she regained her balance. The shoulders of her cloak were saturated, and she sneezed. The heavy cloud combined with the twilight to produce early darkness. Again she slipped. She could hardly see and that wasn't only because of the poor visibility; she was so utterly tired that her eyes were only half open.

She would have been in bed now if she had remained at the manor. Don't think of it . . . Remember Captain Ridgeway . . . He had befriended her . . . He deserved to be well received in his own neighbourhood . . .

Her hood was sodden and clung to her forehead, her feet were wet and her ankles muddy. How much farther was it to the Red Lion? Half a mile?

Her foot slipped on the squelchy ground, her hands flailed the air as she tried to regain an upright stance. Her left foot slid farther into the narrow rut left by a farm tumbril. Trying to prevent herself from falling she twisted her ankle and in the next moment's agony all thought was suspended. All she knew was a sickening pain and then she felt herself slipping backwards.

There was total darkness.

Her next conscious thought was that someone was pouring water out of a jug close to her ear, which didn't make sense. Of course, it couldn't be that; it must be Mrs Panton pouring another cup of tea.

She opened her eyes but everything was grey and vague. Then memory returned as water dripped off the beech leaves on to her face and rain splashed into the puddle beside her. She had fallen, but she must get to the Red Lion. She tried to sit up, a torturous pain from her foot shot up her leg; she thought she was going to be sick and lay back hastily. The nausea passed but she was so exhausted that she had no desire to move. She was actually grateful for the refreshing feeling of rain on her skin and the sweet smell of damp grass near her nose.

This was foolish. She had to move but when she put even the slightest pressure on her foot the pain was so acute that she knew she couldn't stand. How could she get to the Red Lion?

Why should she try? Fred and Maggie's old cottage was very near. True, it was very dilapidated and must be letting in the rain badly. The roofless upstairs was probably nearly as wet as this ground but the downstairs would be protected by the bedroom floor. If she could crawl that far, she would gain shelter until it was time for the mail coach to arrive. That must be some hours yet and she might be able to walk by then.

She dragged herself with difficulty along the ground for some yards and then groping along the earth her hand encountered a long stick, her fingers closed over it and she felt that her problem was solved.

With its aid she eased herself up and hobbled the short distance to the deserted cottage.

In the darkness its decrepit condition was not so obvious and as she entered it she felt it offered her security. A tinderbox and a candle would have been useful, but it was unlikely that the Colts would have left anything behind them.

She sneezed violently and removed her saturated cloak. It had protected her well, for her hair was dry, but the lower skirts of her gown were wet. She literally wrang the cloak out and the water dripped on to the floor, which was made of beaten earth. The Colts' old home was not nearly so comfortable as their new cottage. The place smelt musty and was probably the home of mice and bats. There was no sign in the gloom of a chair. Her eyes became accustomed to the darkness and she found it wasn't total; she could look round the bare interior and felt sure she would see a chair if there was one. As she had expected, Fred had removed all they possessed.

All? There was something in the corner;

on closer inspection it proved to be a heap of sacks with an old blanket and a cushion which appeared to do duty as a pillow. She supposed that Fred had left some bedding behind him, deciding that it was worthless.

She sat on the floor, her skirts spread out around her, her foot throbbing painfully. Her cloak would make a clean mattress, but it was still sopping wet. However, she was so utterly fatigued that she closed her eyes and fell asleep almost simultaneously.

She didn't know why she awoke later, but she supposed it was due to sheer physical discomfort. The floor felt as hard as iron and her whole body ached. The throbbing in her foot had stopped but when she tried to move it into a different position it was painful.

The darkness was not so intense and when she listened she could no longer hear the rain. At most, it could only be a drizzle now and there must be a break in the cloud, for moonlight penetrated fitfully through the broken window.

She was suddenly startled by a bang and then a scraping which could only be made by someone trying to push the outer door wide open, the swollen wood making the task difficult. Clare lay rigid, her heart beating so quickly that she nearly coughed. Straining her ears, she lay perfectly still, with her coppery hair loose about her shoulders and her pale print gown crumpled around her legs.

A distinct grunting sound followed. The intruder could hardly be human. She relaxed slightly and the door of the little room burst open.

The apparition which entered was so strange that at first she thought it was some weird animal. Among the shadows in this dark room it seemed to be walking on four legs and to have a head covered in unkempt hair which partly hid the face and gave it the appearance of some variety of primate.

A second look showed that this was a false impression. The face confronting her was certainly human, although the mass of thick, untidy hair and the unshaven cheeks and chin combined to give it a bestial air. Moreover, the man was crawling on his hands and knees while

149

making the grunting noises she had heard previously.

He stopped suddenly and stared, then slowly stood erect and then lurched drunkenly towards what must be his own bed, for he evidently knew it was there.

It was then that she realised that this must be the character locally known as Daft Harry. She recalled that Mr Ridgeway had described him as a dangerous lunatic, but Mr Bromley believed him to be just a simpleton and harmless. Whatever his mental capacity, he was drunk; his breath smelt of the liquor. This acting on an inferior intelligence might well be dangerous.

She had to get out of his range, but so unobtrusively that he was not fully cognisant of the presence of another human being.

She moved silently sideways, but as she turned her foot the sharp pain caused an involuntary cry.

Instantly Harry's attention became riveted upon her. He came towards her with a queer loping gait and promptly knelt beside her. His eyes were cloudy and bloodshot, his breath rancid. He began to feel this unexpected intruder as though to ascertain what sort of creature had come into his home. His fingers, large and calloused, explored. He pulled her hair, traced the line of her shoulder, felt her cheeks and nose in his big, damp hand. Then suddenly he jerked her towards him.

She was pinioned between him and the floor, unable to move.

Clare gave a terrified scream.

It was not an appeal for help, since she could expect none in this isolated place; it was an instinctive cry of terror.

Physically imprisoned, she also withdrew mentally into a small inner world because reality was too terrifying. So she never heard the loud voice which called, "She's here, Fred!"

Everything which happened then occurred with such rapidity that she was not sure how it was effected. All she knew was that one moment she was pinned to the ground with a strange hirsute face bending over her; the next she was free.

In front of her Jerry, wearing a long, dark coat with several shoulder capes and a beaver hat pulled forward on his head, gave a final kick to the prostrate form of Daft Harry which now lay near the door through which Fred Colt was just entering the room.

"I've been rather rough with him," Jerry was saying. "You may have to patch him up a bit."

"All right, sir. You leave 'im to me. 'E's probably quite 'armless really."

"Probably, but he terrified her. I'll take her down to the lane, where I left the phaeton, and send my groom to help you with him."

Clare struggled to sit up, which was very difficult because her injured foot was underneath her. At least she could see better now. Jerry took a large lantern and held it nearer to her. "What's happened, Clare? Can't you stand?"

"I twisted my foot and then I couldn't walk. That's why I came in here. But I found a stick and used it to lean on. It must be somewhere here."

"You'll have to lean on me instead of a stick. Come on!" He put out his hand and drew her to her feet. "Your gown feels wet. Where's your cloak?"

She pointed to it, finding difficulty in speaking as she began to shiver feverishly.

"There? It's saturated. Here, wear this." He swung his own caped coat off his shoulders and put it round her despite her protests. "Now for the phaeton. You've had a shock and you've been soaked. No wonder you're shivering."

"I was only frightened for a few minutes," she said, ashamed now of the fear his presence had removed.

"Possibly, but you've been wet through for hours. Let's get home."

"I can't go back to the manor."

"Oh, yes, you can and stop thinking about that letter you received."

How did he know? But she felt too weak to ask. Even treading lightly on her sprained foot was painful and although the coat hanging heavily from her shoulders had stopped her shivering, she felt hot and cold by turns.

He offered her his arm, but she hesitated. Her foot nearly let her down and she winced but tried not to show how much it hurt.

"If you don't take my arm, I shall give

you a piggyback and that would be most undignified!" he teased.

She smiled gratefully and put her hand into the crook of his arm. By the time they reached the door she was really leaning on him.

He gave Fred some directions and left him the lantern. When they emerged from the cottage the damp air met her; Clare began to shiver again despite her borrowed coat. The rain had cleared away but drops splashed on them from the overhanging beech trees as they walked down the lane, and Jerry's boots left big footprints in the rain-sodden earth.

Clare felt so weak she could hardly think.

"Your shoes are soaked through," Jerry said. "I hope you've got webbed feet."

He admitted to himself that it wasn't much of a joke, but he wanted to chase away the memory of that ugly moment when she had been at the mercy of poor Daft Harry. She was usually very responsive to the slightest touch of humour but there was no reply. He turned to look at her as she kept silently limping beside him. She hardly knew where she was and yet he didn't think she was afraid any more. She was shaking; she'd got a feverish chill, and no wonder.

Clare was barely conscious of anything; only vaguely aware of being handed up into the phaeton. Out of habit she smiled and mechanically thanked him. When Jerry asked if she was all right she answered that she was quite comfortable, thank you; but she didn't know what she had said.

When they entered the drive, he drove past the laurels and the rhododendrons, then into the stableyard. She was only just conscious when he tossed the reins to a groom, jumped to the cobbles, lifted her down and carried her into the house by a side-door. In the light of a lamp left burning on a table he saw the thick hair rioting over his black capes, with the auburn and copper glints glowing. Mrs Panton came hurrying to meet him, her black skirts rustling. She opened her mouth to exclaim in relief that he had found Clare and horror at the girl's exhausted condition.

Jerry silenced her with a look and

said in a low voice, "I've already had to take two grooms into my confidence. That's enough. Clare isn't likely to want everyone to know where she went tonight, nor the reason for it. I'll carry her upstairs. Get her some hot milk, Panny. She's feverish."

He carried her up to the first-floor landing, where he hesitated, considering taking her into one of the bedrooms where she would be more comfortable than in the servants' quarters. Then he decided against that. If she awoke later in the night, still febrile and in unusual surroundings, she might be very confused. He turned to the narrower flight of stairs which led to the attic storey and bore his burden into the little room allotted to her.

Mrs Panton collected a bowl of warm water and when she entered the room she saw that he had removed his heavy coat and was laying a hand on Clare's brow.

"Is her forehead hot?" asked Mrs Panton anxiously.

"Burning. It's very obvious that she has a fever."

"And no wonder! Just look at the

lower half of her skirt. That child's been drenched. I'll have to take that gown off. Go out of the room, sir, whilst I sponge her down and put a clean bedgown on."

"Can you manage?"

"Easily."

He went out, wearing his heavy coat slung over his shoulders.

Clare was vaguely aware of the reassuring presence of Mrs Panton as her clothes were pulled over her head. She was rubbed down with a cloth soaked in cool, sweet-scented water. Then one of the lace-trimmed bedgowns which her mother had made for her years previously was dragged from her carpet-bag and put on her.

Again instinctively, Clare kept murmuring words of gratitude. She shook her hair free and Mrs Panton made no suggestion of putting a nightcap on it.

When Jerry returned she was lying in bed. She was still flushed but no longer hot — quite the reverse.

Clare shook so much that the bed began shaking, too. Her teeth chattered, she sneezed and turned over still shaking uncontrollably. Jerry looked at her anxiously and then said with apparent irrelevance, "Panny, pull my boots off."

His hessians fitted so perfectly that he certainly couldn't have removed them unaided and he was determined not to waken his valet. The fewer people who were roused the better. (The grooms already knew that Clare had been out alone and brought back exhausted, although they didn't know why she had gone out in such inclement weather.) The housekeeper struggled successfully with the boots and then stood them in a corner.

She disappeared for a few moments and returned with some hot milk. Jerry was just taking off his coat, which he put over the back of a chair. Clare tossed and turned, her hair flowed over the pillow and strands became entangled in the lace of her bedgown. She murmured something incoherent and clutched at the sheet with a feverish hand.

"She'll have all the bedcovers off, and she's frozen as it is," pronounced Mrs Panton anxiously.

"I know." Jerry came to the other

side of the bed. Together they raised the trembling girl and Jerry supported her while Mrs Panton held the cup to her lips. But Clare was still too ill to understand what was required of her.

"Drink it up, there's a good girl." Jerry's voice was firm and commanding. It penetrated to her consciousness and Clare began to drink.

When the milk was finished Mrs Panton said, "Thank God for that."

"Amen," said Jerry and gently laid Clare down again. He pulled the covers up closely and she lay quiescent for a while.

Then the shivering started again and she whimpered in her uneasy half-sleep.

To Mrs Panton's amazement Jerry promptly stretched himself full-length on the bed and pulled Clare into his arms, deftly tucking the covers round her and holding her very close to him. The shaking began to abate.

"I could keep her warm, sir."

"I know, but I can do it better. I shall hold her tightly. She will fall out of bed if she continues to toss, you know."

159

"It's not fair to keep you awake, sir. It's my job."

"Good Lor'! I've had many a full night awake. Have you ever been on board ship in a storm? Of course you haven't! Nor tried to slip through a French harbour in the darkness! I thrive on staying awake."

"We could take it in turns, sir."

"Where am I?" asked a bewildered voice.

"You're all right, Clare. You're safely at home," said Jerry reassuringly.

"I haven't got a home. Where am I?"

"Hush, Clare. I'm here — Jeremy Ridgeway. Go to sleep."

Something consoling in his voice must have soothed her but full understanding had not yet returned. "Don't leave me," said Clare but her eyes stared uncomprehendingly at him.

"Of course I shan't leave you. I shall stay here all night." The shivering stopped; she laid her head on his chest.

Jerry looked over his shoulder. "And you'll stay here all night, Panny, too. I'm sorry, but it would ruin this child's reputation if anyone were to discover that

160

I lay on the bed beside her throughout the night with no one else in the room."

"I understand, sir."

"Can you make yourself comfortable in that chair? There's no need to stay awake. I shan't hurt her, you know."

"Of course I know, sir."

Jerry smoothed Clare's hair back from her forehead and then drew her even more closely into his arms.

Mrs Panton watched them, straining her eyes in the darkness. The captain's tall figure in shirt and breeches took up the entire length of the small bed. The girl in his arms was still and quiet now. Mrs Panton thought how natural they looked — the slim figure with the long hair and the lace collar more than half concealed in the captain's embrace.

"Can you go to sleep, Mrs Panton?"

"I think so, sir." She pulled a shawl round her shoulders. "But it doesn't seem right — you having to stay awake all night."

"I'm not going to do. If she wakes, I shall feel her stir and that will waken me. I reckon we can all three sleep for a while now. Goodnight, Panny, and thank you."

Mrs Panton yawned. "Goodnight, sir."

Outside, an owl hooted. Inside, the housekeeper smiled as she heard the deep, regular breathing which told her that Jerry was already asleep.

9

JERRY swung himself into the saddle outside the new home of Fred Colt. Three ducks stood beside the open door waiting for Maggie to feed them. Fred's scythe lay where he had tossed it in the long grass. The swallows dived from their mud nests under the eaves and flew across the teasels in the front garden. Jerry waved a cheerful farewell and the rhythmic beat of Columbine's hooves pounded on the grass as he cantered past the oak tree where ivy clustered, and the narrow stream where gnats swarmed.

In the tall grass beside the ditch grew a profusion of buttercups interspersed with dead nettles, clover and ribwort plantain. A young starling flew over the hawthorn hedge and from some high but hidden perch among the trees a cuckoo called.

Jerry reached the stableyard and entered the house with his determined stride going straight to the library, where he found his grandfather wearing a mulberry coloured coat.

"You're up earlier than I expected, sir."

"And you were later than I expected! Where's Clare? I woke early and began to work out a little chess problem for her. Tell her to leave whatever Mrs Panton's told her to do and come here."

"She can't. She's in bed and — "

"In bed! Whatever for?"

"She contracted a chill through being out in that heavy rain last night."

"Silly girl! She shouldn't have gone out."

Jerry sat on the drum-top table and idly played with the thong of his riding-whip which he had absentmindedly brought into the room. "I want the whole truth about Clare Winster."

Mr Ridgeway looked at him thoughtfully and then felt in his pocket for his snuff-box. He offered it to Jerry, who shook his head but bent forward to examine the little box, which was composed of Sèvres panels painted with cherubs and mounted *en cage* in gold.

"What an extremely unsuitable thing

164

for you to own! You bear no resemblance to a cherub. I'll give you a more appropriate one than that which I bought in a Baltic port. Now, about Clare — "

"What's it like?" asked Mr Ridgeway eagerly.

"What?"

"The snuff-box you're going to give me."

"You greedy old devil!" laughed Jerry. "I'll go upstairs and get it for you when you've told me what I want to know."

"I'll tell you what I know; but what was Clare doing last night? Having an assignation with some young man?" From under his heavy brows he watched an expression of annoyance cross his grandson's face.

"Nonsense!" retorted Jerry sharply. "She received a letter."

"So that was it. I suppose one of the village lads wrote it asking for a meeting. I'll wager half of it was misspelt. It would be if he was one of those who went to Dame Tilson's school. The woman can't spell correctly herself."

"It was nothing of the kind! Clare

wouldn't go running off to the first ignorant loony who sent her a note."

"There's no need to rip up at me but I suppose it's only natural that you should try and protect her. Ironical, though." The old gentleman's voice dropped, his chin sank into the folds of his neckcloth as he added almost to himself, "After all, she might be your sister."

Jerry wheeled round, his dark eyes dilated, and, tugging furiously at the thong of his riding-whip, he demanded, "Oh, my God! She isn't, is she? She can't be! Tell me she isn't!"

"She isn't."

"Are you sure?"

"Absolutely. Use your intelligence, boy. Does she look like any Ridgeway you've ever seen?"

"No. She's a damned sight better looking than any of us."

"Speak for yourself!" retorted his grandfather and eyed the agitated jerking of the riding-whip. "I'll tell you everything if you put that thing down. It looks very menacing."

Jerry gave a reluctant laugh and dropped the offending article on to the sofa. "Go on, tell me."

"You're always so quick to defend your father. But if I tell you the truth I don't think we shall quarrel. We might have done once but not now." In spite of this remark he looked up apprehensively.

Jerry smiled reassuringly. "No, sir, we shall not quarrel. But I don't promise to accept your interpretation of the facts whatever they are."

"That's your decision, but I'm afraid they're only open to one interpretation." The old man stared down at Horatio sleeping peacefully on the floor.

Jerry watched the strong light turn Mr Ridgeway's hair to a silvery white. His eyebrows were drawn together in a frown, creasing his forehead. At moments of stress he looked his age. "A glass of grog?"

"You naval men! Yes, I'll take one, thank you."

Jerry poured out two drinks and replaced the stopper in the crystal decanter. He held out a glass to his grandparent and sat down. "Well?"

Mr Ridgeway took a drink and put down his glass. Then he began his narrative. "If you are to understand about Clare Winster's origins, then I must explain to you certain things which occurred several years before you were born. As you know, Crewe's land marched with mine even prior to the enclosure and from the time that it became obvious that he would never have a son he and I planned to unite the properties eventually through the marriage of my son and his daughter Isabella."

Jerry guessed that his father had refused to espouse the girl. "I suppose neither of you thought that they might not like to live together. What comfort is a vast estate if you're not happy with your partner?"

"A lot of comfort, I should think!" observed Mr Ridgeway tersely. "As usual, you are jumping to defend your father before you know the facts. He said he thought it was a good idea, which isn't surprising for Isabella Crewe was a lovely young woman. She didn't have Clare's green eyes but she had more colour in her cheeks and her hair was just as pretty."

"Do you mean — ?"

"Wait a moment. Let me finish."

Jerry tried to be patient.

"Jeremiah seemed so well satisfied that we used to allow them to go walking about the grounds of Crewe Hall together alone. Crewe and I often watched them from the library window. Their heads were close together as if in earnest conversation. Then off they would go into the little temple where the gardeners kept their tools. I have since wondered if that's how the trouble started. I presume your father, who never could learn tact or discretion, took liberties which annoyed her. Probably she wasn't prepared to indulge him and very likely he drew the conclusion that she was cold and lost interest in her. I don't know. All I do know is that two days — two days," he repeated, "before the wedding he jilted her. Can you imagine how I felt? We already had guests staying in both houses. The insult to the Crewes was intolerable. It is hardly any wonder that Titus broke off all intercourse between our families for some time. Later, we were forced to communicate about local matters but all warmth and understanding had gone."

For a moment there was silence. The

expression on Mr Ridgeway's face told Jerry that even now the old gentleman had not recovered from the acute embarrassment he had suffered. The event must have occurred.

"And Isabella?" he prompted.

"Broken-hearted. She couldn't bear people to look pityingly at her. In a month she had run off and married her father's head gardener. Crewe disinherited her but he blamed the Ridgeways for causing her such pain that she eloped with the one person who seemed to understand her. He set up a nursery garden somewhere in Chelsea and that's where Clare was born. She knows she's related to the Crewes but she doesn't know what your father did; Isabella was too good-natured to tell her. I know you think I was too implacable towards your father, but consider what he did to me."

The old man looked broodingly out of the window and his dark eyes glistened.

Jerry said, "Thank you for telling me; I can see it hurt." Then with a characteristic return to joviality he said, "I'll fetch your box now. You've earned it!" He dropped a hand on his grandfather's shoulder and gripped it for a moment, then hurried from the room.

He was back quickly.

"There you are." He opened his fingers placing something in the old gentleman's hand.

Mr Ridgeway held it to the light and for a whole minute was quite speechless. It was a brown enamel box, oval in shape, its lid embellished with a small plaque depicting a baying hound surrounded by a circlet of diamonds.

"For me?" he asked with an almost childlike simplicity.

Jerry nodded. "If you like it. The maker's mark is underneath. It originated in Petersburg. The Russians make some pretty things of that sort."

"But it's valuable, my boy."

"Aye; it's too good for that abominable snuff you offered me. Where do you get it? It's as dry as dust. I suggest you let me buy you something better in the Haymarket next time I'm in London."

Mr Ridgeway fondled the box. "It's exquisite. Are you sure you don't want to keep it?"

"Good God, no! I can't abide snuff.

171

Makes me sneeze."

"That's because you take too much at once."

"Probably, but I prefer a cigar."

"Such a dirty habit," reproved his grandfather. "If you must have those, I hope you'll smoke them in the garden."

"Oh, I will — when I'm not smoking them in the library!"

Their eyes met; Jerry's brimful of humour, his grandfather's frankly affectionate. But it was not in Mr Ridgeway's nature to indulge in sentimental reflections. He said brusquely, "Get out the games table and set out the chessmen — not that I shall enjoy the game. You could play well if you tried, but you don't stick at it. You have sudden bursts of inspiration, make one or two brilliant moves and then you lose interest."

"I know. I forget one can't attack in line astern on a chessboard!"

"I used to play with Crewe before we quarrelled but even when we began to talk to one another again we didn't revert to our old relationship although the enclosure certainly improved matters.

People don't offend Titus Crewe with impunity."

Jerry placed the pieces of carved bone in position on the board. There were several further questions he wanted to ask about Clare, but he judged that the old man had found the subject a strain and decided to postpone his queries. But he was dissatisfied that Isabella's daughter should be scrubbing Mr Ridgeway's floors. Several times during the game he frowned and once he made an unpremeditated move with his knight which he instantly regretted.

★ ★ ★

"Here's a bowl of Flemish soup which Mrs Scorby has sent up for you, Clare. How do you feel now?" Mrs Panton came into the room.

Clare sat up in bed. "Much better, thank you. I'm quite well enough to get up and do some work."

"You can get up and go into the garden but you're not to work today."

Clare was puzzled. When she had awoken some hours ago she had felt more comfortable and secure than at any time since her mother died. She had shut her eyes again and it felt just as though a pair of strong arms encircling her relaxed their hold. She was so sleepy she didn't think about it for a moment and then, as she opened her eyes once more she could have sworn she saw Captain Ridgeway slipping out of the room with a pair of boots in his hand. Had she suffered from hallucinations?

"Mrs Panton; last night — was I alone?"

"No. You were so ill that two of us stayed with you until you awoke much better this morning."

Then it was true! She hastily swallowed some soup and burnt her throat. No wonder Mrs Panton had not said who the other person was! But Clare knew perfectly well that Captain Ridgeway was only being kind. He had probably saved her from getting an inflammation of the lungs.

She said hastily, "Last night's raincloud has disappeared."

"Yes, there's blue sky this afternoon. You can take a turn in the garden."

In the early afternoon while the sun was nearly overhead Clare slipped out of doors. She passed a border of pinks and admired the purple-blue of Canterbury bells while the perfume of carnations wafted towards her. An enormous bee crawled across the centre of a marigold; the cedar tree cast its shade over the lawn and small white clouds like tufts of raw wool swept overhead.

A thick, tall yew hedge on her left shielded part of the rose garden where Jerry strode with his hands in his pockets whistling 'The Banks of the Nile'.

He turned and saw Clare coming down the path. It was apparent that she hadn't seen him yet.

He ceased whistling and began to sing in a deep, rich voice:

"Your waist it is too slender and your fingers are too fine . . . "

She stopped and listened. As she approached the sundial she suddenly saw him and sank into a curtsy.

"I hurried out and so I'm afraid I didn't put on my cap."

"Thank God for that!" he said fervently and the twinkle in his eyes reassured her.

The red tide ebbed from her face and she began to thank him again for rescuing her from Daft Harry. He terminated her speech by drawing her attention to the antics of Horatio, whose floppy ears lifted and fell in time to his excited barking.

"I think it's my fault that Horatio has brought the blacksmith's dog here," confessed Clare. "I gave your dog a bone and he is so gallant that he went and brought his lady friend, so I gave her one, too."

"Quite right, Horatio," said Jerry, laughing. "You should always share your food with your lady love. Clare, I want you to dine with us tonight. The Bromleys are coming and we've no hostess."

She tried to disconnect his previous remark from this invitation, remembering she was only a housemaid. "I'm extremely grateful to you for giving me the opportunity of dining with you but it wouldn't be suitable. I'm a servant here."

"Then it's part of your duties! Clare, Mrs Panton told me that you had received a disturbing letter last night and that you had left a note to say you were leaving. She presumed you would go to get the mail coach but the downpour was so bad just after you had left that she concluded you must have sought shelter before reaching the Red Lion — possibly with the Colts."

"So that's how you knew!"

"Yes. And when you weren't at their home, he and I decided that you were sheltering in the ruined cottage."

An insect alighted on his shoulder and instinctively she put up her hand to brush it off his coat. Not what a housemaid should do. Whatever must he think? She was withdrawing her hand hastily when he caught it and held it, looking down at the long, slender fingers, their skin roughened by housework.

"No more scrubbing floors!" he commanded.

"It's my job."

He shook his head. "I'll tell Panny to engage another housemaid to share your duties. You haven't time to do them all; you're wanted to play chess. I gave my grandfather a game and made a terrible mistake."

"Your bishop?"

"No, I won!"

"Oh dear!"

"I was thinking of something else and I forgot to leave him a loophole. He was checkmate and I'm in disgrace!"

They leant against the sundial and laughed.

Clare was the first to stop. She said, "I can't dine with you when the Bromleys come. I should be imposing upon your grandfather."

Jerry seemed amused. "Nonsense, my dear! No one imposes upon my grandparent. If there's any imposing to be done, he does it himself!" He turned his head to regard her penetratingly. "Who put such an idea into your head? Crewe?"

She looked amazed at his perception.

Jerry said, "I can see that he did. I have just discovered that your mother was his daughter. Were you, perhaps, trying to take refuge at Crewe Hall when you disappeared last night?"

"Oh, no!"

"But you were going to leave us."

"I didn't want to do so." The words

178

came out on an impulse.

"Titus Crewe suggested it, eh?"

"He thinks your grandfather took me in because his conscience told him to do so."

"Most unlikely! What a pair of grandfathers we've got! Mine's an old devil but he's a likeable old devil with a few redeeming qualities. For yours, I'm sorry to say, I have nothing but contempt. Ignore Crewe. He's trying to make you feel guilty so that you'll leave. Has he asked you to live with him?"

"No."

"I thought as much. He will be aware that this neighbourhood will think it very wrong of him to allow his granddaughter to work as a maid in another household, when he ought to be looking after her himself. The cunning old fox is trying to goad you into leaving us simply to spare him from embarrassment. Don't succumb to his persuasions."

"You're very kind. If you're sure you wish me to do so, I will come down to dinner tonight."

"I'd be grateful. I thought we ought to invite the Bromleys but the old gentleman didn't trouble to organise a proper dinner for them, just asked them to come and take pot luck with us. Those were his words. Poor Mrs Scorby! Stay here at the manor, Clare. Remember you're an adornment to the place."

"I should be glad to stay."

"I think my family owes yours something anyway. I induced my grandfather to tell me this morning just why he is so bitter against my father. It's not a reason I particularly want to dwell upon, but if I don't tell you what it is, I shall feel that I address you every day under false pretences."

She couldn't imagine why but she knew that the usually confident and careless Jerry was genuinely embarrassed. In an uncharacteristically sombre voice he recounted quite simply the facts concerning the engagement between his father and her mother many years previously and how it was broken. "Your mother lived away from the protection of her family for the rest of her life. I know that you were very fond of her, so that I felt in all honesty I ought to tell you this."

Jerry would always have a deep affection for his father's memory. It was evident that they had been close to one another when Jerry was a small boy. Mr Ridgeway's revelations could not destroy such filial affection but they had shocked the captain. Intuitively, Clare understood that he had been badly hurt and that he didn't really want to tell her the truth about his father's behaviour; but he had done so.

A pigeon cooed near the dovecote and the wind blew Clare's hair forward, half hiding the green eyes as she replied slowly, "My mother only once mentioned your father in my hearing and then she called him, 'One of the greatest gentlemen of my acquaintance.' Whatever she felt about him, it wasn't resentment. I can't blame him if she didn't."

He said nothing but he gave her a look which thanked her and he raised her hand to his lips.

A light gust of wind scattered lupin seeds, shook the bergamot and ruffled Clare's copper curls. "Thank you for telling me." She curtsied and hurried down the path, past the pink and crimson china roses towards the house. She wouldn't stay talking any longer lest he thought that she was presuming upon the friendliness he had shown towards an employee in his grandfather's house.

She offered her assistance to Mrs Scorby and took a tureen into the dining-room and stopped in front of the portrait of the second Jeremiah. His hair was powdered, his forehead was wide and beneath it a pair of black eyes seemed to be fixed upon her. She was convinced that the artist had portrayed them faithfully, because they were not merely typical Ridgeway eyes — very dark and intelligent — they had a character of their own. Humour lurked in them but they didn't have the sparkle which animated Jerry's.

The longcase clock struck and the lacquered bracket clock promptly chimed as well. Five minutes later the ebony pedestal clock announced the hour. That would annoy Mr Ridgeway; he couldn't abide timepieces which were not accurate. Then the ormolu clock in the library chimed quarter past the hour. Mr Ridgeway entered the hall with his gold watch in his hand.

"Hedges!" he shouted.

"Sir." The butler emerged holding a soft cloth.

"Whatever are you doing?"

"Burnishing the epergne, sir."

"I don't mean that, you fool! I mean what are you about to allow every clock in the house to register a different time? You're negligent — that's your trouble. You can stay up tonight until three o'clock. That's when the mail coach passes the drive end. It's always punctual to the minute. You'd better wait down there at the lodge gates and take that Dutch carriage clock with you. Set it correctly to three o'clock, bring it back here and put the others right."

"May I venture to suggest, sir — ?"

"You may not venture to suggest anything. And don't stand there wringing that cloth in your hands; you look like Lady Macbeth." Then, feeling in a better humour for his outburst, he added, "Out, out, damned spot!"

Hedges, who was not familiar with the works of Shakespeare, took this as a personal attack and withdrew hastily but with dignity.

Clare hurried to the kitchen. Mrs Scorby was taking great pains with the food.

"Here, Betsy! Whip up these egg whites and then get me those pears which Clare candied for me. Oh, here she is! Are you better, love?"

"Yes, thank you."

Mrs Scorby delicately placed crystallised violets in the cream edging of the pie.

Clare looked at the spit turning in front of the fire where Betsy was basting a piece of beef. "I thought you were going to use a leg of lamb."

"Don't speak to me about legs of lamb. That wretched dog, 'Oratio, 'as been and took it. And when I told Captain Ridgeway all 'e did was laugh. I reckon 'e's proud 'cos that dog's such a good thief. And don't you pretend you're not trying to laugh yourself, Clare Winster, 'cos I can tell by your eyes. Betsy, stop basting that meat and start whipping them eggs!" ordered Mrs Scorby. "I'll be needing them soon. There's a dozen of them in that bowl on the dresser.

The whites 'ave been separated already. 'Urry up!"

Betsy's face was red from the heat of the fire. She turned round dripping hot fat from the basting spoon.

Clare said, "I'll whip the eggs."

She had just started to do so when the captain came unexpectedly into the kitchen. He sat on the corner of the immense table and began to help himself from a pile of currants and raisins beside Mrs Scorby's mixing bowl.

He looked around him as though very interested in the string of onions hanging from the ceiling, the pair of ducks not yet plucked but intended as part of tomorrow's dinner, and the assortment of jellies shuddering slightly as Clare whipped the egg whites nearby. He said as casually as he could do, "Mrs Scorby, you were here when my father was a young man, weren't you?"

"Don't you remind me of my age, Master Jeremy. Yes, I was but I was only young myself." She was fifty this summer and she didn't want Betsy to know it. The sixteen-year-old girl thought that people who had attained their fortieth birthday were ready for the grave.

Jerry put a handful of currants in his mouth and chewed them abstractedly before he asked, "Did he come into the kitchen and pinch things like I do?"

"No, he didn't! But he was a real friendly man, all the same. Always passed the time of day if he saw anyone around the house."

Jerry took an apple and bit it meditatively. "When his engagement was broken, did he seem very upset?"

Mrs Scorby paused in the act of squeezing a lemon and looked at him shrewdly. "Your dad was like you. If 'e was upset about something 'e wouldn't let nobody know."

Jerry made a grimace and changed the subject abruptly. "Clare will be having dinner with us. I sent a message to Hedges that an extra cover was to be laid."

"Clare!" said the cook peremptorily. "Put down those egg whites. You'll 'ave ter go and change if you're to eat dinner in the dining-room. You can't sit down in a working-gown and apron. Mr Ridgeway'd 'ave a fit."

Clare went upstairs, carrying a larger ewer of water. As she stood in her little attic, rubbing a towel over her naked body, she almost forgot her menial role in the household. She was going to wear the gown she had so meticulously stitched in her spare hours. When she came down the top flight of stairs to the broad landing she noticed that one of the bedroom doors was open and crept in to survey herself in the cheval glass.

Her hair newly washed and left in loose curls, was only adorned by a narrow blue ribbon. The low, square neck of her gown revealed her pale skin and the slight train emphasised the grace with which she walked, while the open robe disclosed the delicately embroidered petticoat. She went rather shyly downstairs to where the gentlemen were awaiting the arrival of their guests. They turned towards her. She didn't hear the quick intake of Jerry's breath but she saw approval in his eyes.

He wore a black velvet coat, which was absolutely plain, even the buttons being covered in the same material. It was worn over a plain satin waistcoat. His light-coloured knee-breeches, white stockings and black pumps pleased his grandfather's hawklike gaze. The old gentleman leant on a gold-knobbed cane and wore a wine red velvet coat with an old-fashioned lace jabot at his throat.

He put up his quizzing-glass to survey the embarrassed Clare and said with surprising gentleness, "You look very well, my dear."

The visitors arrived very promptly and would have been early if Aurelia Bromley had not insisted that the carriage should stop for a few moments at the lodge gates to ensure that they did not look too eager.

Mr Bromley was clearly delighted because he had been asked to dine at the manor. He rubbed his plump hands together and spoke in a very hearty voice. "Well, well! This is very pleasant. If this is pot luck, sir, we are very lucky. Eh, my love?" He dug his wife in the ribs with his elbow and then beamed on his host. "I'm glad you wanted to ask us to a family dinner. That's real friendship, isn't it?"

Mr Ridgeway had not intended it to be anything of the kind. His hand, as he lowered himself into the chair at the head of the table, shook slightly.

Jerry intervened hastily. "I have a feeling harvest is going to be late this year. There's been a fair amount of wet weather."

Mrs Bromley pronounced gloomily, "There's not much point in having a good harvest because the French will come and get it."

"Quite frankly, ma'am, I don't believe that Bonaparte will jump the ditch now," said Jerry.

"You want to listen to this young man, my dear," advised Mr Bromley jovially. "He's accounted for one of Boney's gunboats himself, whilst it was on its way to Boulogne. He even brought one of the Frogs' boats out of its anchorage. I give you all a toast. The Audacious Captain!"

Jerry looked acutely uncomfortable. The effusive comments confirmed Mr Ridgeway in his belief that George Bromley was a vulgar person, but he glowed with silent pride in his grandson. Clare wanted to hear more about Jerry's exploits but she also wanted even more to alleviate his embarrassment. As everyone lifted their crystal glasses, she tried to think of some way to divert attention from him. She succeeded by getting Mrs Bromley to talk about her offspring. Jerry threw her a grateful look.

"I hear that Roger is learning to ride, ma'am," said Clare.

"Yes. I expect he'll fall and break his neck while we are away — if not worse. We have to go north, where my sister needs my support in her confinement; she is very near her time. And George has to visit the mill. Roger will be left alone and his tiresome nurse cannot look after him, as she has contracted influenza in the summer of all times. I am distracted with worry."

"Bring him here," suggested Jerry. "Clare will look after him." He thought it would be more suitable for her than scrubbing floors.

"Now if that isn't real neighbourly of you!" exclaimed Mr Bromley. "Are you sure you don't mind?" he asked Mr Ridgeway.

"I don't suppose the boy will be any worse than Jerry was at his age. If these two can keep him out of my way, I shall contrive," said Mr Ridgeway consuming roast ribs of beef and asparagus tossed in butter.

Candlelight twinkled on the cut glass and on the gilded picture frames. Clare noticed that Jerry's gaze strayed several times to the portrait of his father and she wished that he had never been told of what Jeremiah Ridgeway had done.

The gentlemen stood up politely when the ladies withdrew.

Conversation with Aurelia Bromley did not prove difficult, as the guest talked almost without cessation. She was afraid that Roger would have a fatal riding accident, that Luddites would burn down her husband's mill, that she would be unable to find a decent chimney-sweep in Dunnock Green and she didn't believe that the danger of an invasion was over.

The door opened and the gentlemen entered the room. The superior port which had been passed round the table had enabled Mr Ridgeway to view his guest with more tolerance, but it had increased Mr Bromley's confidence. Mr Ridgeway lost some of his amiability when the guest offered his arm.

"I'm not in my dotage yet. I don't need to lean on any man and when I want an arm, I'll use Jerry's."

"Quite so," agreed Mr Bromley affably. "Indeed, sir, I think you're wonderful for your age."

This phrase did not mollify his host, who grunted audibly. Mr Bromley sat with his podgy hands folded across his stomach. He found the small teacup difficult to hold and the warmth from a fire in the summertime excessive but what did that matter? He was a guest at the manor and he would be able to tell other people that he had been invited there. He watched the captain kick a log into a blaze and then smile down at Clare Winster. Twice it seemed as though some joke passed silently between them. It occurred to George Bromley that it might be possible now to restore his standing with Mr Crewe. He had obviously offended that remote gentleman by referring to his granddaughter being employed as a maid.

No matter; he would go at the first opportunity to Crewe Hall and admit that he had been mistaken in her menial status. On the contrary, he would assure Mr Crewe that Clare Winster was regarded as a lady and highly favoured by the gentlemen at Ridgeway Manor.

Yes, he could tell Titus Crewe all about it now, he reflected happily, as he observed the captain give one of Miss Winster's curls a playful flick with his finger.

10

THEY were playing skittles outside the Red Lion when Mr Bromley rode back from Crewe Hall with a bewildered expression as if he didn't know whether the news he had just delivered was good or bad. But no one saw him go past.

Bill Brown was puffing at a clay pipe and watching the contestants. Against the background of dull thuds as the ball struck the ninepins, Fred told Bill, "Maggie's much better. T'other night when we 'ad all that rain not a drop of water came in our cottage."

"I expect that's why her cough's better."

"Aye; though it could be that stuff Clare brought her from the 'pothecary. I remember Clare's ma at the same age. She was a lovely girl, but I reckon Clare's 'air is a nicer colour."

Fred added "You'd think 'er grandad would be ashamed that she 'ad to go and work at the manor. If I ad a bonny granddaughter, I'd want to look after 'er myself. Not 'im, though. 'E don't mind letting Mr Ridgeway feed 'er and that."

A shadow fell across Fred. He glanced over his shoulder to see who had come up so quietly behind him and gazed straight into the pale countenance of Titus Crewe. Immediately his own face reddened. Mr Crewe had that effect upon folk; he didn't say anything, he simply fixed an accusing stare upon them and the most innocent people, who had no idea how they had offended him, felt instantly guilty.

"It is always unwise, Colt, to utter sentiments in a public place unless you know that what you are saying is absolutely accurate. On this occasion it is not. I have no doubt that you are going to be extremely sorry that you made such an ill-informed comment."

Many men quailed if they just saw Mr Crewe advancing towards them but Fred wasn't like that.

He retorted, "I don't know nothing about ill-informed comments. All I know is that Clare Winster's your granddaughter and she 'asn't got no 'ome. There's plenty of rooms at Crewe 'All, isn't there?"

Even he was frightened after that. Mr Crewe did not say anything for a moment; he simply looked at Fred, beginning with the man's untidy hair and slowly lowering his gaze to include the sweat-stained shirt, the shapeless trousers tied at the knee with cord and the old boots more scuffed at the toes than ever.

In the awful silence Fred had ample opportunity to study Mr Crewe — not that he wanted to do so but there seemed nowhere else to look. The gentleman's skin was as white as if it were winter, his pale eyes like the glassy green of a cold sea. His coat was made of grey whipcord and his waistcoat of pearl-coloured cloth. His whole appearance was as pale as a layer of thin cloud.

"Your insolence will not be forgotten. There is no room in our nation for those who are a liability to it, but there is space in Van Diemen's Land where such people can be given the opportunity to labour usefully and hard."

The menace in his voice underlined the threat of transportation which he had just uttered. Despite the hot day Fred felt a cold sensation grip his stomach. To be transported for seven year's penal servitude to the colonies would part him from Maggie — possibly for ever, because he would never be able to afford the fare for the voyage home. He had certainly not committed any crime for which that was the accepted punishment, but the warning in Crewe's icy gaze was unmistakable.

The gentleman turned and walked away with dignity, rebuked the blameless groom who was leading his horse, and rode off to the vicarage. He intended to cause extreme discomfort to the Reverend Daniel Anson, who had the temerity the previous Sunday to preach a sermon on the text: 'It is easier for a camel to go through the eye of a needle than for a rich man to enter into the Kingdom of God.' Mr Crewe did not normally attend divine worship and, if this was a sample of what the incumbent was teaching his foolish flock, then Titus Crewe would speak most forcefully to the bishop.

"Bloody bastard!" exclaimed Bill Brown, but he waited until Mr Crewe was out of earshot before saying it. "You'll 'ave ter take care, Fred. 'E'll 'ave you for something."

Two days later Clare went to see Maggie. Alice from the village was being employed to scrub and Roger Bromley wasn't due until the next day. It was very hot as she wandered down the field path. She stopped to speak to Brown Bess, the old bay pony which Jerry had given to Fred after purchasing it from a travelling tinker who spoke of slaughtering it.

Immediately Clare entered the small cottage she knew something was wrong. Maggie's eyes were reddened and her lids swollen.

"What's the matter?" asked Clare without preamble.

"I know it's silly of me," said Maggie. "It could 'ave been much worse. Lots of folks wouldn't mind but Fred's not like that. I suppose people think we're just rough, but Fred 'as 'is pride. Mebbe a young man would think it was funny, but Fred won't laugh. The trouble is folks are bound to come and stare just because no one's been in there for ages."

"I don't understand. Where is Fred?"

"You mean you don't know? I thought that was why you'd come, 'cos I knew you'd be along to comfort me once you 'eard about it."

"Please explain," said Clare and sat on a stool to listen.

Maggie's narrative was disjointed and long. Clare found it difficult to unravel, but it transpired that Brown Bess had been discovered in one of Mr Crewe's fields which bordered the lane near the boundary of the Ridgeway land where Hawthorn Cottage was situated. Fred had been certain that the gate was securely shut; moreover, Brown Bess was not particularly energetic, nor prone to stray. However, she was found trespassing and, because he owned her, Fred was held responsible. To penalise him the constable had locked him in the stocks.

"But I don't believe that's the real reason, miss," declared Maggie with conviction.

"It certainly seems a harsh punishment."

"It's wot 'appened to Will Thomas when his 'orse strayed on to Mr

Ridgeway's land. But that was twenty years ago and no one did it to Ben Felton when 'e let all 'is pigs on to parson's croft — and that weren't no accident!"

"Then why has this been done to Fred?"

Maggie was evasive. "Mr Crewe don't like 'im 'cos of something Fred said about 'im."

Clare waited to be told what it was, but Maggie remained silent.

Clare murmured something sympathetic and Maggie wiped away a tear with her sleeve. "Will you take this bread and cheese to 'im, miss? I'd go meself although it'd set me off coughing, but that's not the problem. It's just that I think 'e'd rather I didn't see 'im sitting there with folks jeering at him and 'im not able to do anything about it 'isself. 'E's always been one to use his fists has Fred. It don't seem right for 'im to be fastened up."

Clare gave Maggie a sympathetic kiss and took the hunk of home-made bread and the slab of cheese wrapped in a piece of butter muslin. A short while ago Maggie couldn't have afforded the cheese but Fred now had a regular wage from Mr Ridgeway.

Clare walked quickly down the lane, thinking that Fred's life had always been hard. She recalled the things he and Maggie had told her without any self-pity. As a very small boy Fred had been employed long hours in the fields by a local farmer to scare off the rooks, using a wooden rattle, a labour for which he received threepence a day. Later, when he was old enough, he would go to the hiring fair each Michaelmas. He never got a job with a tied cottage and when he married Maggie he had little to offer her except his devotion and his physical strength.

Maggie was the youngest and weakest of a very large family. 'The runt of the litter' had been her father's description of her. But somehow Maggie had survived and when she was seventeen she began work for the farmer who was currently employing Fred as a labourer. She earned sixpence a day for removing stones from the soil, picking them up individually and placing them in the basket she carried as she made her arduous way, bent nearly double, across the sticky earth. Even then there was a sweetness in her face which attracted the healthy, clumsy Fred. They were married at Easter and the villagers marvelled at the gentleness with which the big man treated his delicate wife. "Like an ox protecting a lamb," someone said. Fred might be rough in his appearance and speech but he looked after Maggie, refusing to allow her to continue her back-breaking job.

But he couldn't always find work himself. They grew accustomed to being the recipients of parish relief. He would have loved boys of his own but no children were born to them. Perhaps it was just as well, for Maggie's delicate body might not have survived childbirth. Perhaps that was why Fred became so fond of Jerry. People used to watch the large peasant with his rough speech holding the hand of a small boy, who plied him with continuous questions in an eager, educated voice.

And then Jerry went away to sea. Subsequently the enclosure robbed Fred of his last semblance of a living — no longer able to keep a cow on the common or a pig in his garden, he was even evicted from his shabby dwelling.

Yet he wouldn't admit defeat. He refused to accept that he and Maggie should enter the workhouse. He chopped down trees on forbidden territory and thatched the crude shelter. Sometimes when the wind shook it he wondered if he had done right. Ought he to have taken her to the confines of the workhouse, which was built to be weatherproof? But at night when they lay down in privacy together he decided that no one should deprive him of his liberty. And they hadn't . . .

. . . until now.

As Clare emerged from the shade of the overhanging trees into the dazzling sunlight which spread across the village green she heard raucous shouts.

A group of people hid her view. She joined them and insinuated her way between a woman in a sunbonnet and a small boy sucking a toffee apple. Then she got her first sight of the stocks with the whipping-post attached to them. Fred was imprisoned between the two wooden bars, his legs encased in decrepit boots and firmly locked in the slots.

He tried not to wince when an apple core hit him.

The ground was still rather damp from the rain of two days before. The tension in the muscles of his calves was becoming painful. He attempted to shift his position, placing his hands flat on the ground and endeavouring to transfer some of his weight to them.

His frayed trousers, the knees neatly darned by Maggie, were stained green from the damp grass.

There had once been a wooden bench for prisoners to sit on but this had rotted and been removed.

It was a long time since the stocks had been used. The curious hurried to the green.

"I must go and 'ave a look. I've never seen anyone in the stocks."

"No more 'ave I. Wait a minute, Dick, and I'll come with you."

"There's that lad of Robinsons with a load er stuff to throw at 'im. Look, Dick!"

The curly-haired youth disapproved.

"It ain't fair. Wot's Fred Colt done to 'im? All the Robinsons is the same and Will 'Arris there would throw mud at 'is own ma if she was in them stocks."

Fred's shoulders sagged. Life in his primitive dwelling had accustomed him to enduring all weathers but it had caused stiffness and a premature stoop. Yet above the bowed shoulders he kept his head erect. It ached from the heat and the tension of remaining still, even when he expected to be struck at any moment and from any direction. As he braced himself, a stick with a sharp bud hit the left side of his face and a trickle of blood began to course down his cheek from a small cut on his temple.

Two boys ran up, carrying between them a wooden bucket containing dirty water. "Let's throw it over 'im just for a lark!"

"No, it's not fair. Poor feller!"

"Come on! Pour it all over 'im!"

Fred's fingers clenched and his lined face showed strain. He tried to contain his anger, for he had lost enough of what dignity a poor man possessed.

Clare ran up to the boys, her eyes

bright with anger. "No! How can you? Have you no more courage than to attack a defenceless man?"

One youth looked sheepish. "It's all right, love; we're not going to touch 'im."

The other one with a cheeky grin added, "But we don't mind touching you."

His friend became bolder. He thrust his head forward to leer at Clare while he gave a shout of strident laughter. "I fancy you, love," he declared.

"You can 'ave your choice, love. Either we'll pour this over 'im or you can come behind the haystack with us."

Clare pushed the bucket and overturned it, drenching the grass. She dodged the arm outstretched to grasp hers and hurried across to the constable, who was standing unhappily under a large chestnut tree. The boys loped off towards the pond to refill the bucket. Clare didn't notice them; she was persuading the constable to give the bread and cheese to Fred. Then she drew back into the crowd, thankful that she was below average height, for she didn't want Colt to notice her; he would be more miserable if he knew that she had seen his indignity.

She glanced anxiously forwards, her face half hidden between the brawny arm of a man in a frieze coat and the lanky figure of a spotty youth who suddenly shouted something derogatory. His yell was piercing and Clare instinctively put her hands over her ears. The obscene screech had drawn Fred's unwilling attention and he turned in Clare's direction. Even at this short distance she could see the stricken look of hurt pride in his eyes.

Pushing her way through the press of villagers she lifted her skirts above her ankles and began to run in the direction of Ridgeway Manor.

Since her only thought was to reach Captain Ridgeway as soon as possible she was glad her ankle was better. She ran lightly and speedily, like a fawn, but the heat made her gasp, her throat became sore and she was breathless when she dashed into the house.

Harold Thompson, a farmer who rented land from Mr Ridgeway, was in the library talking to his landlord and to the captain. He was looking apprehensively at his gaiters and hoping that none of the damp soil adhering to them would drop on to the carpet.

Clare didn't wait for permission to enter; she flung open the door and rushed in, clutching her shawl round her shoulders over which her coppery hair rioted in untamed curls. The cap she had been wearing had dropped off somewhere along the field path. She wasn't even aware of the exact words by which she addressed the captain as she ran across the long room towards him.

"Jerry! Jerry! Can you come? It's Fred Colt. I don't know how to help him. Can you do something, please?"

"Good God! What is the matter?" Jerry took a quick step towards her and caught the dishevelled Clare in his arms.

Mr Ridgeway paused in the act of taking a pinch of snuff and surveyed the pair with curiosity in his dark eyes and a slightly amused smile on his narrow lips.

Clare was so out of breath that she found it difficult to gasp out the vital information. "It's Fred."

"Is he ill?"

"Not exactly but he will be if — " She caught her breath and her chest heaved. It was dreadful that now she had reached a source of help she was unable to get out the words.

"Steady, Clare. Get your breath back."

The captain's strong, supporting arm round her waist was comforting. Then she felt his fingers sorting out her curls and smoothing the long hair. Mr Thompson's eyes grew positively round. He hadn't witnessed anything so interesting since Toby Harris tried to drive a flock of forty sheep through the turnpike whilst only paying for twenty.

Clare regained her breath and told Jerry the facts succinctly finishing with the anxious question, "Can you do anything about it?"

"Yes," he answered shortly. He pulled the bell-rope. "Hedges! Send a message to the stables. I want Columbine saddled at once."

"Yes, sir."

"I must bid you good-day, Thompson." Jerry took long strides across the room and flung open the door.

Mr Ridgeway looked up at him. "What are you going to do, Jerry?"

"Do? I'm going to get Fred Colt out of the stocks."

Mr Ridgeway said, "I suppose it's no use my telling you that you're a fool?"

"None!" laughed Jerry.

Clare swung round to face the old gentleman. "He's not a fool!"

Mr Ridgeway chuckled from the depths of his armchair. "Little vixen!"

"Follow me, Clare," ordered Jerry over his shoulder. "Don't stay to be abused."

As the door shut behind them Mr Ridgeway said in an uncharacteristically confiding way, "You know, Thompson, I begin to think that I used to lead a very dull life."

"It is kind of you to concern yourself about Colt, sir."

"Oh, I don't. I'm not concerned about him at all. But if my grandson likes to entertain himself I shan't try to stop him. I shouldn't succeed anyway," he added to himself.

Clare hastened out of the house. It would take time for them to bring

Columbine round and Jerry had gone upstairs to change into riding-breeches and top boots. She could tell Fred that help was coming.

But she did not get there first. Jerry had been very quick, so had the groom. She heard the thud of Columbine's hooves behind her as she reached the end of the lane and Captain Ridgeway passed her at a canter, slowing as he reached the green. She hurried up behind him.

Jerry rode quickly on to the green; the mare's hooves churned the ground while ducks, geese and stragglers from the crowd scattered hastily. He reined in his horse, surveyed the scene and listened to the jeering youths who surrounded the stocks, yelling and shouting in excitement.

A tall boy picked up a fistful of mud which he hurled at Fred. It struck his cheek and plastered it with oozing brown. The boy danced up and down on the spot. "I've hit him! Look! I've scored a bull's-eye. I can aim better than you, Ned Smart!"

Jerry lips tightened into a thin, straight

line. He raised his right arm.

Whoosh!

The boy's cry of triumph turned into a howl of pain as Jerry's riding-crop hit him hard between the shoulderblades.

There was a gasp from the onlookers while the boy doubled up momentarily, conscious only of a searing pain across his back. Clare stared incredulously at Jerry, hardly able to believe that this seething man was Captain Ridgeway. Jerry's face was livid with fury and his black eyes blazed.

There were cries of alarm and suddenly the knot of boys broke up. They dispersed in all directions and cottage doors banged around the village green as frightened lads sought refuge.

Nell, a plump woman wearing a calico apron, looked up at the irate captain. "You done right, sir. 'Tis a pity their parents don't teach 'em 'ow to behave proper."

She was ignored.

"Fetch the constable!" Jerry rapped out the order.

The man came up reluctantly, shuffling his feet in the grass. In trepidation he faced Captain Ridgeway.

"Why is this man in the stocks?"

"Well, sir, Mr Crewe told me to put him in there."

"Is Mr Crewe a justice of the peace?"

"No sir, but — "

"There aren't any buts. Has Colt been before the magistrates? Did they condemn him to sit in the stocks?"

"No, sir."

"Let him out!"

"But, sir, Mr Crewe — "

"Damn Mr Crewe! I told you to release him."

"Yes, sir, but — "The constable looked miserable.

"You don't know whose orders to carry out, eh? If you understand what's good for you, I'm the one you'll obey!"

Hearing Jerry's 'quarterdeck voice' the constable had no further doubts. And if he had had, one glance at Jerry's eyes would have removed them.

He unlocked the stocks and raised the upper bar. Fred had some difficulty getting up after so long in a cramped position. Numbness in his feet was succeeded by a prickling sensation and he was compelled reluctantly to cling to the constable, who put a sympathetic arm round his shoulders. It was shaken off. "I can manage," said Fred gruffly.

"I'm sorry," said the constable his rubicund face redder than ever. "I didn't want to do it."

"I know," admitted the victim. "It weren't really your fault. Crewe forced you."

Columbine shied nervously when the upper bar of the stocks slipped back into its normal position with a bang. Jerry tightened his reins and spoke to the constable. "In future if Crewe gives you orders, you will refer them to me and I will tell you whether or not to obey them."

"Yes, sir," said the constable with abject compliance although Jerry had no authority to issue such a directive.

Clare had recoiled with shock when she heard the crack of Jerry's whip. For a moment she had covered her eyes, then she retreated to the shadow cast by the boughs of the chestnut. Now, as she saw Fred actually walking away a free man, the stiffness went out of her body and with a deep sigh of relief she hastened forward.

"Thank you, sir," Fred said looking up at Jerry.

"No need to thank me. It was Clare who told me what had happened. But for her I should still be at the manor."

Embarrassed at receiving thanks she thought were undeserved Clare asked Fred, "Has the constable given you your food? Maggie sent it."

"Yes, love, thank you. But I'll go and set her mind at rest now." Looking at the man on horseback he added, "Captain, I'm glad you're back in the village."

Jerry smiled. "Go home and forget the incident if you can." He turned to Clare, saw the bewilderment in her white face, and explained, "Crewe is an evil man. He won't soil his own hands with mud or blood; he just creates a situation in which a few insensitive lads can pretend to be tough and important. I despise a man who can brutalise ignorant boys. I don't want to flog the village lads but I'm damned if I'll sit by and watch them ill-treat others."

"Wasn't there anything else you could

have done?" asked Clare unhappily.

"Possibly. I'm afraid you've seen the Ridgeway temper today."

She glanced up and found he looked quite wretched. She didn't say anything and there was disappointment on his tanned features. Instinctively she put out her hand towards him. He took it and his fingers interlocked with hers.

When she withdrew her hand and hurried away, the vicar came up riding a sturdy cob. A few people still talked excitedly on the green but many hastened off to find someone to whom they could recount the whole tale. One went to tell the blacksmith, who had been shoeing the horse belonging to Titus Crewe's bailiff. A couple ran off to the fields to describe to the haymakers how the captain had made the constable disobey Mr Crewe, besides giving Will Harris a lesson he wouldn't forget.

"I 'ope Mr Crewe don't take it out of the constable 'cos 'e's let Fred out," said the curly-haired youth.

"'E won't, Dick. The captain won't let 'im."

"Mebbe not," Dick swung a stick

moodily. "But I don't trust that Crewe. 'E's a bloody rat."

Daniel Anson turned to the captain. "Did you hear what Jack said?"

"Yes. He's evidently a young gentleman of discerning judgment!"

11

WHEN his horse had been shod, the bailiff rode to Crewe Hall to tell his employer that he couldn't get the rent owed by Medley, who pleaded high prices, numerous children and disease among his poultry. It might be wiser not to mention this at once and perhaps it would be judicious to describe the drama enacted on the green if it took Titus Crewe's mind off the delayed payment.

It did. Mr Crewe was so interested that he thanked his employee for trying to obtain the rent.

The bailiff stood stiffly in front of the desk.

"So the village boys amused themselves at Colt's expense, did they?" prompted Mr Crewe.

"Most of them."

"Most of them?"

"The majority did but they stopped very quickly when they saw what happened to young Harris."

"I am not aware of anyone called Harris. A chicken-hearted boy, perhaps?"

"Not exactly, sir; anyway, there was no point in staying any longer."

The deep eyelids veiled the expression in Titus Crewe's eyes. "Why not?"

"By then Colt had been released."

"Released?" Mr Crewe raised his head and looked directly into Grayson's eyes as though accusing him of something, although the uneasy bailiff couldn't imagine what.

"Are you telling me that Colt is no longer in the stocks?"

"Yes, sir."

"The constable has taken it upon himself to liberate the man?"

"No, sir. He was only obeying Captain Ridgeway's orders."

"Explain what you mean."

Grayson began with an energetic recital of the activities of the local lads and the anger of the captain. When he recounted the constable's total capitulation to Captain Ridgeway he became aware of the chilling look cast at him by his one-man audience. He paused for a moment and ended with the admission, "Of course I didn't see or hear any of it myself. The people who told me may have exaggerated."

"Precisely. One should always discount the ramblings of rustic gossips. You may go, Grayson."

The bailiff was deflated and couldn't get to the door quickly enough, but when he reached it his employer's voice detained him. "One moment, Grayson. I require you to collect the outstanding rent from Medley. Remind him that it is a debt and that I do not intend to retain a tenant who does not pay what is due."

"Yes, sir — I mean, no, sir."

The bailiff disappeared and Mr Crewe sat at his desk in silence. He couldn't reconcile the description just given him with his brief sight of Jeremy Ridgeway pushing a barrow and joking with his grandfather's maid and a penniless yokel. Now he was being asked to believe that the youthful populace and even the village constable were afraid of the captain.

He frowned and gazed abstractedly

out of the window towards Dunnock Green, taunted by his memories. From here he could just see the little Doric pavilion where Isabella used to meet her fiancé. Jeremiah Ridgeway had always appeared good-humoured (although far too high-spirited) and then suddenly he had behaved with callous disregard for the Crewes. Perhaps Grayson had not exaggerated in saying that the captain had commanded the constable to disobey Titus Crewe. After all, he was used to receiving implicit obedience on a ship where he was the ultimate authority.

In vengeful mood Mr Crewe determined to discover what Jeremy Ridgeway cared for most and to deprive him of it. In anyone else such a malicious thought might be short-lived but when he made a resolution he pursued it relentlessly.

The light was strong; he shut his eyes against it. Immediately he saw again the captain laughing while his gaze rested on the slight figure of a girl with coppery hair and green eyes sitting on a barrow.

A very slight smile moved Mr Crewe's mouth into a crooked shape.

The following morning the Bromleys

brought Roger to the manor, and his mother delivered him to Clare with many admonitions. He was not to get in the way of Mr Ridgeway or shout loudly; he hadn't to stroke Horatio when 'that dog' was asleep or he would be bitten; he was to do as Clare told him not forgetting to say 'Thank you' whenever appropriate, and must not scratch the spot on his nose. Finally, Mrs Bromley looked disapprovingly at the captain (Jerry's shoulders were shaking with silent laughter) and said that Roger was not to be put on the back of any horse too big for him.

In a loud voice Mr Ridgeway remarked to Clare, "God grant me patience! The woman's a lunatic!"

Mr Bromley turned with a smile on his chubby face and said, "We are indebted to you, sir, for your condescension in having our youngster here. Didn't I say to you last night, my love, 'Ridgeway's been a good friend to me'?"

"It was Jerry's idea, not mine," answered Mr Ridgeway gruffly. For Clare's ear alone he added, "I wouldn't have been such a fool as to suggest it."

When their carriage finally rumbled away down the drive, a chuckle from Jerry drew Roger's attention and he demanded to be told all about fighting Napoleon and how many French sailors the captain had personally dispatched.

"When you frown your eyebrows nearly touch each other, like Mr Ridgeway's. Why are you frowning, Captain Ridgeway?"

"Because I prefer pulling Frenchmen out of the sea. A lot of them have got boys your age and they want to go home to them."

"I never thought of that. Won't you tell me anything about the navy, then, Captain Ridgeway?"

"Come here then and I suggest you call me Uncle Jerry. It's less of a mouthful."

Roger went to lean over his shoulder while Jerry showed his chronometer, turning it over to indicate the maker's signature on the movement. Roger bounced up and down interpolating questions.

Mr Ridgeway knew little of his grandson's career in the fleet. After Trafalgar he had studied the casualty list in *The Times* and sighed with relief because Jerry's name was not on it. He was glad that Roger asked so many questions. But no one listening could have imagined that after Trafalgar Jerry's face was black, his body aching from top to toe, his epaulette shot away and blood running down his cheek as he limped to the companionway and went down below to forbid the surgeon to amputate the leg of a seaman whose limb might yet be saved. Despite Roger's questions Jerry gave no hint of his part in the battle. One might have thought he had not been there until he made his sole reference to the aftermath of the action.

"When I saw Lord Collingwood's flag flying from the *Victory* as commander of the fleet, I knew Nelson was dead and I felt sick in my stomach."

The piping voice asked, "Did you all talk about the battle for days?"

Jerry shook his head. "Everyone was too tired and there's not much point in boasting about your part in a fight when everyone else has done just as much. There's not much to laugh at either when some of your friends have been killed. We just got to work repairing the damage." He gave a very deep sigh and suddenly looked older. Then he tweaked Roger's ear playfully. "I'll take you fishing tomorrow."

When the boy went off with Clare, Mr Ridgeway tried to keep his grandson talking about his career. Jerry only sketched the bare facts of his rise from midshipman to captain of a second-rate. He was fortunate, he said, to have been midshipman in a small frigate, for it enabled him to be noticed by the captain and recommended for promotion to lieutenant after the minimum period of service required. He gave no hint of the intrepidity and expert seamanship he showed, merely observing that, luckily, he was a junior lieutenant on a flagship so the admiral noticed him and that was why he received command of a sloop. He said nothing of his daring raids on the French estuaries in this vessel. According to Jerry, it was luck that he was subsequently given command of a frigate and he glossed over the fact that a year spent in independent attacks on enemy ships earned him command of a ship-of-the-line and caused him to be the youngest captain at Trafalgar.

However, Mr Ridgeway succeeded in obtaining a few details of an incident in which two enemy ships had attacked the *Rainbow*. "Fired at you from that distance, did they? What did they hope to achieve?"

"They probably hoped to drive us off."

"But you stayed to defeat them, eh?"

"The wind changed two points, so I was able to weather them and bring them to close action while cutting them off from their own shore."

Mr Ridgeway chuckled with delight. "And you defeated both French ships?"

Jerry was anxious to keep to an accurate version of the event. "We maintained a fight for some hours. We disabled one completely and he struck to us. The other hived off with the loss of his mizzen topmast and his fore-top-gallant."

Mr Ridgeway rubbed his hands together with satisfaction.

12

ON Sunday Clare went to church, where she sat in the squire's pew with Roger and Captain Ridgeway.

A shaft of sunlight, penetrating through the stained-glass window, tinted the grey pillar with shades of ruby, emerald and amethyst whilst it highlighted the alabaster features of Thomas Ridgeway, who lay in chain mail beside his lady.

Clare was glad to join in the words which always inspired her. She was accustomed to the use of an organ in a London church but such a modern notion had not touched Dunnock Green where the small village band centred on Hubert Strutt, who played the bassoon.

Roger's gaze was fixed on the serpent, a cornet eight feet long, which was twisted in snakelike curves and produced an impressive low note. The little boy was so fascinated that he stood with his back to the pulpit and stared at the gallery in the west end of the church, where the choir and village band were located. Dick Miller played the flute, his cheeks round and roseate; as the psalm proceeded, the singers and players became more conscious of the hot weather. Beads of perspiration dripped from Dick's forehead while Bill Webster, manfully blowing into the serpent, had developed a bulbous countenance and his balding head glowed.

As Daniel Anson's earnest voice intoned the familiar prayers, and Clare knelt with closed eyes, she put out her hand to take Roger's in a comforting clasp. She felt a responsive pressure on her own hand, firm and reassuring, but the fingers which squeezed hers were not the small ones belonging to Roger. He had slipped to the other end of the pew, where he was putting the prayer books into a tidy pile. It was Captain Ridgeway who held Clare's hand.

The next day he insisted that she should come when he took Roger bird-watching beside the river. The boy was excited when she brought a picnic basket. She wore one of her old gowns, a pale yellow, with her hair in a topknot from which the long copper curls hung in graceful ringlets on to her shoulders.

They passed the mill, where water gushed over the rotating wheel, and took a field path between clumps of sweet-smelling balsam to a stile which led them to a secluded path along the river bank. They had to stop and wait when Roger climbed a tree where he got stuck and had to be rescued by Jerry. A swan glided with smooth elegance downstream. The tranquil water was green with the reflections of overhanging trees and crossed by silver ripples. Two cattle from the far bank stepped ponderously into the water.

"Look, Clare! There's a cow paddling! I'm going to paddle."

And soon Clare sat beside the willows with a small pair of buckled shoes and some white stockings at her side. She became pleasantly drowsy and then stretched out full-length on the river bank. Overhead the sky was a cloudless blue. The breeze shook the branches of a willow which swept the water with its pendulous leaves. Insects visited wild flowers, which grew among the grass and scented the ground on which Clare lay.

She heard a splash when a fish jumped in the water and the high-pitched voice of Roger asking a ceaseless string of questions and the deeper tones of Jerry answering him. Tufts of marsh marigolds grew by the river's edge, where Roger and Jerry were talking about otters and woodpeckers. Clare rolled over on to her side, their voices became indistinct and she fell asleep.

The next thing she knew was an hour later when someone said, "Wake up, Green Eyes!"

She looked up and saw Jerry bending over her dangling a bunch of ripe cherries. "Bite!" he invited.

She did and giggled and nearly swallowed the stone. He tickled her cheek with a blade of grass, she squirmed delightedly and Jerry's face came closer to hers.

"Clare! We saw a kingfisher. Did you see the kingfisher?"

Jerry drew back and muttered something under his breath.

"No, Roger, I didn't." Clare sat up.

"And Horatio went swimming in the river and when he came back he shook himself and the water went all over Uncle Jerry and me. Uncle Jerry used a bad word."

Clare laughed. She lay back in the grass utterly relaxed, with her coppery hair tumbled about her shoulders. The topknot had come undone and a long curling strand blew across her cheek. Jerry touched it lightly and moved it aside.

She said shyly, "It's just as well if it covers the freckles."

"No, it isn't. Freckles can be very attractive, Clare Winster. Take my word for it!"

"Come and look for the kingfisher!" urged Roger, getting hold of her hand and tugging hard. She sat up again, tossing her hair back over her shoulders, got to her feet, then brushed seeds and bits of grass from her crumpled skirts.

They walked to the edge of the bank and sat for a long time with no sight of the bird, although Roger insisted that they would see it if they waited long enough. Clare watched the inverted image of the swan upon the rippling water. A coot made its erratic progress downstream and the branch of a small tree was carried past them on the current among the cool reflections of the green boughs.

"Look!" The little boy pointed eagerly.

Jerry, who was chewing a blade of grass, nodded and drew Clare further forward, indicating where she should look. She was at first more conscious of his hand on her arm and the proximity of his face to hers than she was of anything of ornithological interest. But she obeyed the unspoken command to look at the stump of a willow tree. Perching on it, the plumage of its breast brick-red in the sunlight, was the kingfisher.

In his excitement Roger moved too suddenly and, with a flash of iridescent blue, the bird flew over the water to disappear into a hole in the opposite bank.

"It will have a home full of fishbones," said Jerry.

"I'm hungry," said Roger.

"It will soon be your bedtime," said Clare, conscious that the sun was low in the west, its light gilding the ripening corn and casting the shadows of trees over the meadow. With reluctance they moved away and Roger, sitting astride Jerry's shoulders, shouted gleefully, "Gee-up!" as they approached the house.

Mr Ridgeway came into the hall to meet them. "You're back at last!"

"Don't say you missed us, because I won't believe it!" teased Jerry.

Roger was still sitting on the captain's shoulders when they turned to go through the library door, so Jerry had to stoop so that his 'rider' did not bang his head on the lintel. This delighted the youngster, who declared it was just like riding a real horse. Jerry gave a commendable whinny and then 'threw' his rider on to the sofa amid shrieks of enjoyment.

Mr Ridgeway lifted a letter from the desk and handed it to his grandson. "This was brought from the Receiving Office."

Jerry broke the seal, scanned the contents rapidly and pursed his lips in a silent whistle.

Roger was bouncing up and down on the sofa. He caught Jerry's arm. "Can we go fishing tomorrow? Mr Ridgeway,

Uncle Jerry caught a big fish and he's going to ask Mrs Scorby to cook it. I'm going to eat it."

"Be quiet, boy! What is it, Jerry?" Mr Ridgeway was studying his grandson's unusually sober face.

"Uncle Jerry, can we go fishing again tomorrow?"

"I'm afraid not, lad." But the captain's eyes were not on Roger. He was looking at Clare, who stayed silently beside the window. As though aware of his intense look she turned.

Their eyes met.

When he spoke, it was to her, as if he had forgotten the presence of the other two.

"I've got to go to London," he said simply.

She nodded and her face was suddenly in shadow as an early evening cloud blotted out the sinking sun.

Jerry pulled the embroidered bell-rope and asked for Mrs Panton. Clare stood tensely by the window and Mr Ridgeway dropped his stick on the floor as he always did when he was agitated. The housekeeper arrived.

"Put Roger to bed, will you, Panny?" asked Jerry.

She curtsied. "Come along, Master Roger."

"No." The child looked mulish. "Clare puts me to bed." He traced a pattern in the carpet with the toe of his shoe and drew back when Mrs Panton tried to take his hand.

"Roger! Bed!" said Jerry sharply.

There was no further hesitation. Roger followed Mrs Panton out of the room.

Jerry glanced distastefully at the letter in his hand.

"There was nothing to pay," said Mr Ridgeway typically.

"I'm sure there wasn't," replied the captain drily. "I presume the Regent is allowed the use of a free frank."

"The Regent?"

"Well, those who write on his behalf."

"Been receiving messages from Royalty, have you?" Mr Ridgeway sounded eager.

"You could call it that. Actually, it's written by some secretary or other. Prinny wants to see me."

"The Prince Regent has asked for you? You mean, you've been invited

to Carlton House? It's a great honour."
Mr Ridgeway actually rubbed his hands
together in satisfaction.

"Not much of an honour. Any captain
would have done — so long as he'd been
at Trafalgar and had a few adventures
since then. It appears that the Regent
wants to hear first-hand accounts from
people who knew Nelson. I just happen
to be on land at the moment."

"At the moment!" echoed Mr Ridgeway
anxiously.

"Oh, I'm staying. I was going to see
them at the Admiralty in any case. I
shall be put on half-pay. But I don't
fancy reliving my battles with Prinny. I
suppose he wants to hear how I blew a
French ship to bits, killing God knows
how many men. We rescued all we could
but it wasn't half of them."

"I thought you were proud to defend
your country."

"I'm willing to do it but I'd rather
shoot Bonaparte in cold blood." He
studied his signet ring thoughtfully and
added, "I am convinced that he will
intensify his efforts to destroy British
trade. If this nation is to win the war,

it will have to be adequately fed with home-produced food. It may not be so exciting to encourage the use of the new threshing-machines as it was to steal into a French harbour and destroy invasion craft but it could be as useful to the country's welfare."

Since Jerry needed to leave so soon, there were many jobs to be done. The next day an argument broke out between Mr Mallow and Mrs Panton. She had helped to look after Master Jeremy when he was a child, but Mallow, as the captain's valet, had every right to attend to all the details concerning the captain's raiment. In the end it was Clare who ironed Jerry's nightshirts while the other two continued their dispute. Jerry walked into the dining-room where he stood looking at the portrait of his father. He thought he was alone and only Clare, passing the open door, saw him. She detected an expression on his face so much at variance with his usual equanimity that she could not forget it.

Everyone dreaded Jerry's departure. "At least he's not going back to his ship," said Mrs Panton when some of the staff congregated in the hall to wish him a good journey. Clare was remembering how Jerry had looked as he bent over her on the river bank clad in riding. breeches, top boots and open-necked shirt. She was therefore astonished at his appearance when he descended the stairs.

He wore the undress uniform of a captain in the Royal Navy. His dark blue coat with its stand-and-fall collar had wide lapels, while light glittered on the gold bullions of his epaulettes. His sword was suspended from a black leather belt which fastened with brass lion's-head buckles. His white breeches were well tailored but instead of the traditional buckled shoes he wore the black hessian boots fashionable among young officers.

Mr Ridgeway looked at him with misty eyes and tried to disguise his pride, but no one was regarding the old gentleman. All eyes were on his grandson. Mrs Panton curtsied and her chatelaine jingled.

Clare was suddenly very conscious of her dark maid's gown with its ruffled collar and the little white cap on the back of her coppery hair. Jerry's correct uniform and his impressive height made him seem awesome and she felt as though she ought to go back to the kitchen at once. She fixed her gaze on one of the three brass buttons on his pocket while she drew back a little and bobbed the sort of quick curtsy expected from a housemaid and still stared at his button because she daren't look up into the face of this man who seemed to be the embodiment of authority until . . .

"Well, Green Eyes?" It was that same teasing voice again.

"I hope you have a good journey, sir," she said demurely but she dared to look up at him and smile.

He grinned. "I shan't be away long." And he added in an earnest tone, "Take care of yourself."

He said goodbye cheerily to the company in general, stepped through the door into the fresh air, put his cocked hat on his head and turned to salute his grandfather. Then he went down the steps with his dark blue coat-tails swinging jauntily and his hand resting lightly on the hilt of his sword.

At first the knowledge that his grandson's company had been requested by the Regent palliated the parting for Mr Ridgeway. He even took pleasure when Roger's parents came to collect him in informing Mr Bromley, "My grandson is away at present. He has been sent for to Carlton House." But at Ridgeway Manor everyone noticed that the old gentleman's appetite had dwindled; he sat over his port with a morose expression on his face, announced that he was crippled with rheumatism and actually gave orders that Horatio was to sleep in his bedchamber during Jerry's absence. When someone tried to banish the dog to the kitchen Mr Ridgeway swore volubly and when Mrs Panton, tidying up, moved Jerry's beaver hat and cane from the hall table, Mr Ridgeway snapped, "Leave them alone, woman! They're not doing you any harm."

Clare, summoned to the library, found him sneezing. He had taken the snuff-box which Jerry had given him out of his pocket twelve times in half an hour just to look at it, but he absentmindedly helped himself to some liberal pinches of the mixture at the same time.

"Jerry doesn't approve of this sort," he told Clare. "He's going to have a special mixture made up for me in the Haymarket."

The old man's hand shook, his head was sunk on his breast and his voice was low as he said, "I don't think I could bear to lose him now."

"Of course you couldn't."

He looked up and his eyes were dull. "I've not always treated him well. In fact, when he was a boy I was too harsh with him."

"Yes, I know."

There was a flash of the Ridgeway fire in the dark eyes. "You're not supposed to agree with me, girl. You ought to tell me I only did my best for the lad."

"You can't expect me to agree with you for beating Jer — Captain Ridgeway."

"That's the whole point, isn't it?" said her employer wearily. "I can't beat Captain Ridgeway in any way. I don't even want to any more. It was a small boy who couldn't defend himself whom I belaboured." He stared into the fire for a moment and then a smile slowly spread over his face. "That's not true. He could defend himself by simply not caring what I did."

Clare nodded, her eyes soft with appreciation of Mr Ridgeway's perceptive understanding of his grandson; although she suspected Jerry had minded sometimes, but if so he wouldn't even allow himself to know it.

13

THE sight of a servant in maroon and silver livery bringing a letter made Clare hold her breath. Before anyone called her she knew it was from Crewe Hall. She took it and went upstairs to read it alone. The folded paper was sealed with red wax and impressed with Titus Crewe's usual signet ring, depicting the snake crushing the life out of a stoat. Clare broke the seal and opened the sheet.

Dear Clare,

I think you will have to forgive me for expressing the opinion that you were most unwise to neglect the well-meant advice I sent to you by a previous letter. Already there are many who remark upon your association with the captain. This cannot be to his advantage. I warned you that if you informed him of your reason for leaving he would be able to persuade you to disbelieve my warning. In his anxiety to spare you embarrassment and because he is a plausible arguer, he succeeded in disabusing your mind of the fear that your presence brought scandal to his name.

I hear that he is at present away. His absence is most opportune as it enables you to redress your previous mistake. You may now leave the vicinity without reference to him. In this way you will make amends to him for the inconvenience you have caused him. He is too gentlemanly to admit that you have been a cause of embarrassment to him, but I was present to see his face colour when your name was mentioned in a rather suggestive manner at the home of a mutual friend of ours. I am sure that if you referred the matter to him he would laugh it off, but do not be deluded by his jocular manner; he is a deeply sensitive man. If I were you, Clare, this is where I should slip quietly out of his life in the conviction that what you are doing is in his best interests.

If you are unable through lack of

money to purchase a ticket on the stage, I should be very happy to pay for it and to give you sufficient money for your other travelling expenses. I do not think any useful purpose can be served by a meeting between us. Simply ask for my secretary, who will have been instructed to give you what you need. I suggest you make for London, but I must stress that if you remain in Dunnock Green I cannot undertake to protect the reputations of the two Ridgeways, which will be ruined locally.

Yours etc.,
T. Crewe

She could not ignore the implied threat in the last sentence; it was a discreet way of saying that if she didn't comply with his suggestion he would personally and subtly ruin the characters of Jerry and the old gentleman. She recognised in this Crewe's method of ridding himself of an unwanted descendant; but she was afraid that the earlier part of the letter was factually accurate. Jerry had reassured her, but perhaps it had only been for her benefit and he had gallantly disguised the awkwardness which he was experiencing. She became convinced of this and determined to leave at once. He might come back any day. She looked at the clock. Quarter past eleven. The stage left at noon.

She finished her work, packed her few possessions into a carpet-bag — not forgetting her mother's workbox. She was determined not to be beholden to the relation who wanted to be rid of her. She would not ask Mr Crewe's secretary for money. She wrote hastily three letters to Mr Ridgeway, Mrs Panton and Mrs Scorby respectively. She couldn't bear to say goodbye to any of them. She gave them to Jack to deliver because he wouldn't ask any questions. Then still full of impetuosity she ran down the drive with a whirl of skirts and long hair and arrived at the Red Lion to book her seat.

She had acted with such haste that she didn't have time to consider if it was for the best until she was sitting in the coach between a young man and an older lady whose plump person exuded heat. Neither gave her any elbow-room and the lady expressed the belief that the journey would be very injurious to her health. "I've not recovered from last time I travelled in this coach. It did something to me, something internal."

After the first stage Clare began to think she might have made a mistake. Jerry had not appeared to be hiding his discomfiture when he had persuaded her to stay. She thought of the way he had squeezed her hand in the pew during a prayer and the expression on his face when he offered her cherries as he leaned over her on the river bank. But of course the captain could have no particular affection for her. He was just being kind.

They changed horses in a market town and entered a well-wooded landscape. The sky was darkening for rain and she began to feel stiff in her confined seat. Then rain lashed the windows and the fat woman said, "I'm glad I made my will before I set out. I had a feeling I ought to do." Clare had used up nearly all her money paying for her seat and at the inn where they spent the night she couldn't sleep at all. Her neck ached and her pillow felt like wood. The bed seemed clean but she began to remember all she had heard of the bedbugs which infested many inns. The thought seemed so horrible that she got up and spent the rest of the night sitting in a wooden chair. In the morning her mouth felt dry and her eyes prickled with sleeplessness. She couldn't afford breakfast and the young man leered at her in an offensive manner. On the whole, she was glad when they reached London.

The stage deposited its passengers at a very busy posting inn but Clare would have to go supperless to bed in the cheapest inn she could find unless she succeeded in obtaining a place in service at once. She actually knocked at one or two houses but she wasn't even allowed across the threshold. When she rapped the copper urn on a well-painted front door a footman opened it and informed her that she should not come to the main entrance. He indicated the gate in the railings which led to the area steps. Her proper place, he said, was at the kitchen. He shut the heavy door at once and she was so disconcerted that she didn't go down to the servants door.

At the next house she went down to the basement, knocked on the kitchen door and waited in the area. A frumpish-looking woman in a black gown answered. Clare explained what she wanted and the only reply she obtained was, "We don't want the likes of you here." The door slammed and Clare's cheeks flamed.

She realised that anyone arriving in the gathering dusk of that summer evening in shabby clothes and asking for a situation appeared to be an immoral character whom no housekeeper would accept.

The first star sparkled in the sky and people were rapidly deserting the streets. Soon she would be alone except for vagrants and felons. She felt for her purse and went to stand under a lamp and check the coins — enough to enable her to stay for one night in a cheap inn. Shadows flitted in and out of doorways and small, ragged figures darted down alleyways. A hot, sweet smell pervaded the locality and reminded Clare of the stalls where hot drinks were sold. She became increasingly conscious of a dark shadow behind her. She thought it had been there when she stood beneath the lamp bracket counting her coins. She hurried to the stall.

The Vendor sold saloop, a very sweet, cheap drink. People surged round him. Clare approached and was promptly thrust aside by a gangly youth whose elbows appeared through the ragged sleeves of his jacket. She fell back and opened her purse, conscious once more of the shadow behind her. She was glad to join the little crowd, for she felt safer there.

Suddenly someone at the back pushed forward and the group swayed and jostled one another. Clare's purse fell from her grasp. She bent to pick it up. Someone trod on her hand and she gave an involuntary cry of pain and lifted her bruised hand to her face. When she looked at the ground again there was no purse to be seen. The shadow behind her had gone.

"My purse!" she exclaimed but no one seemed to hear her although one youth winked at another in the lamplight. Presumably the dark shadow had taken it and apparently he had accomplices. The sweet brew was probably nauseating. Hungry as she was she didn't regret it. The loss of a night's lodging, however, was serious. She wandered away from the stall, penniless, clutching the worn carpet-bag containing her mother's workbox, a couple of shifts and some darned stockings. These were all that she now possessed.

"Past twelve o'clock and a fine night!" The voice of the watch called tonelessly as he came round the corner. Clare decided that it might be wise to keep within earshot of him as he went his rounds. He clutched the railings, trying to regain his breath. A lamp in an iron bracket cast sufficient light for Clare to see him clearly. He wore a brownish-coloured coat with a cape over the shoulders despite the summer evening. He was an elderly man and possibly anticipated rain. The watch took another deep breath, relinquished his grasp of the railings and gave a tug to the shapeless black hat he wore. He pulled the brim farther over his face and started to walk again, leaning on his staff.

As he came nearer he held up his

lantern and she caught a glimpse of a lined face, the chin shaded with a slight grey stubble and the nose rubicund with broken veins. He adjusted the rattle in his hand and lowered his head once more, evidently considering Clare to be harmless. He called out the time again and turned into a road where bow-windowed shops might be a temptation to thieves. Clare heard the tapping of his stick receding in the distance.

She trailed round for the next hour and a half, not always following him but never getting beyond calling distance. His shouted weather reports became more dispirited as it began to drizzle. His voice sounded more tired and evidently he was seeking shelter. The rain began to fall faster and the watch reached his goal — a tall, wooden structure like a narrow box with a gable roof. It didn't look very substantial but the frail shelter would keep him dry. The front of it reminded Clare of a stable door and she saw the old man's head through the open upper half before he leant against the side of it with his elbow resting on the ledge while he dangled his lantern. Lolling against his wooden wall the Charley nodded off to sleep. Clare took shelter in the porch of a church on the opposite side of the street.

Loud voices drew near; she peered out into the darkness and the rain. Shouting, occasionally breaking into discordant song and pushing each other playfully, two men came under the light of an oil-lamp. One nudged the other in the ribs more forcefully than he meant to do. His companion was caught off balance. He lurched against the railings, grabbed a pineapple-shaped finial and shouted drunkenly, "By God! A Charley! Tell you what we'll do, Tom; we'll jusht upshet him a trifle, what?"

Tom's loud laughter echoed in the church porch. "That'sh right. We'll get the best of the Charley."

The watch tried to use his rattle and open his door at the same time. He only succeeded in dropping his lantern, which fell onto the cobbles. The old man was trapped.

"No! No!" Clare screamed but no one noticed her.

The tails of their blue coats flying, the

two bucks ran with long strides towards the Charley's box. One called out that it was a pity they hadn't got a hammer and nails so they could fasten him in it.

Anger welled up inside Clare. She didn't want to draw their attention but this was too much.

"Stop!" she shrieked. "How can you?"

Tom laughed, stood with his hands on his hips and just laughed at her. His friend ran to the back of the box and put both his gloved hands on it, the palms flat against the wood, his fingers splayed out. He gave a violent push and as the box tilted forward he put his booted foot against it and shoved with that as well. The old man gave a cry half of rage, half of fear before his box was thrust towards the road and he was precipitated face downwards onto the hard ground.

Clare, still clutching her carpet-bag, ran forward. "How could you?" she stormed. "Bullying a poor old man is all you dare do!" She bent down and tried to raise the wooden box but she couldn't. "Help me to get him out. He may be hurt."

"George, shall we help the female?"

Tom laughed while the tears ran down his cheeks.

George looked at Clare through bleary and bloodshot eyes. "You have her, Tom, if that's what you want."

"I don't want her."

"Yesh, you do. Jusht shaid so."

Tom swore a blasphemous oath and accused him of lying. He received a blow on the jaw. In a moment they fell upon each other, swaying to and fro locked in combat. They forgot Clare and the watch.

She glanced up and down the street, seeking help in the damp shadows, and then she saw the apothecary's window. She darted across and rapped on the door. Sounds of the altercation continued. But during a pause in the noisy exchange Clare heard footsteps, a bolt slid back and a key turned. The door swung open, revealing the apothecary himself.

He wore an old-fashioned frock-coat and stared with compassionate grey eyes at the shabby girl with the anxious face. "Someone in trouble? Do you want me?"

"It's the watch. He's probably badly

hurt. He was in his box and two young men have pushed it over."

"Couple of peep o'day boys, eh? I'll be along. Just step inside until I get my coat."

She gave a sigh of relief and walked into the shop. The ceiling was low, crossed by oak timbers; the counter was high and supported some brass weighing scales, a glass jar containing a green-striped leech, a silver inkstand with a quill standing in the pen-holder, an account book, a pestle and mortar and several phials containing liquids. Clare read the labels — spirit of lavender, antimonial wine and others. She was glancing at an open case with a red velvet lining containing various instruments when the apothecary returned.

"Now, miss." He took her arm in a reassuring gesture. "Show me where that Charley is."

When they reached the overturned box they found the two young men rolling on the ground, still fighting in a sporadic fashion. The doctor gave each of them a sharp kick and they forgot their quarrel. One complained of being sick and both lay quiescent whilst the apothecary heaved at the simple shelter and Clare glanced back at his doorway where she could read his name — John Bagot.

The watch was dazed, his nose bleeding, and he moaned from the pain in his wrist.

"Let me feel it, Charley." Mr Bagot's large hands were gentle. "You may have broken it. Come along with me. Young lady, you'd better come as well. It's not a fit night for pretty girls to be out on their own."

She thanked him and followed gladly.

Inside the shop there was warmth and Clare took off her wet cloak. The apothecary moved over to a wall lined with small wooden drawers bearing labels to indicate Fine Powder of Bark, Opium Pills, Yellow Basilican and other remedies. He took the glass stopper from a bottle containing Spirit of Sal Volatile. The Charley might need that shortly.

The watch grimly endured the setting of his wrist, fortified by a glass of brandy and comforted by Clare's sympathy; she held his uninjured hand during the process. Mr Bagot observed her white face. When he had finished his professional task he offered the Charley a cup of well-sugared tea and an armchair. He sent his son with a message to the constable to come quickly, apprehend the roistering men and lodge them in the roundhouse.

"Now, young lady, what do we do about you? Take you straight home to your parents, I should think. Sneaking out to meet a young man, eh?"

How much should she tell him? It might be better not to name her grandfather for no application to Mr Crewe would bring assistance. She hadn't to mention the Ridgeways either. Mr Bagot would send her back to them and she would then be a further encumbrance and embarrassment to Jerry.

"I'm an orphan, sir. I came to London hoping to get work. My purse has been stolen but if I can obtain a position as a maid I shall be all right."

Mr Bagot adjusted the gilt-rimmed spectacles on his nose and surveyed her thoughtfully. He was convinced of her honesty.

"You can stay here for the rest of the night and tomorrow I'll take you to Mrs Thornbury. She's a patient of mine and complains that she never has enough good maids." While Clare thanked him Mr Bagot put on his coat again. As he picked up his hat he said, "I'll have to leave you for a while. I've another patient to see. What a night!"

He hastened outside and walked down the dark streets, keeping a wary eye open for any pickpockets. The sky was paler in the east by the time he reached the lodgings where his patient lived.

The sickroom was up two flights of stairs. Under a colourful patchwork quilt lay a man about twenty-five years old; his pallid face touched here and there with a grey shade. A clean bandage was fastened neatly round his brow and above it his brown hair was tousled and damp with sweat. The collar of his nightshirt framed a chin sprouting two days' growth of beard.

He was not alone.

On the back of a chair lay a navy

259

blue coat with brass buttons and the gold epaulettes of a captain. On a small table nearby was a copy of *The Annals of Agriculture*, a pencil and a notebook containing comic sketches of a mongrel. Cluttering the corner of the room was a ponyskin trunk with a caped greatcoat thrown over it, some leather gloves, a case of duelling pistols and a chart of the coastline of Barbados. Beside the window was a cut-glass decanter and a couple of glasses.

Jeremy Ridgeway poured himself a drink and returned to the sketch-pad. He surveyed his latest drawing critically. It depicted the mongrel, nose to the ground, following the trail of some wild creature — a rabbit perhaps — through the woodland. It was Horatio all right except for the tail. He'd got that wrong. He shut his eyes and tried to imagine it correctly.

"I thought they'd have struck by now." The voice from the bed was fretful. "We've no more ammunition. Those damned Frogs should strike now."

Jerry dropped his sketch on to the table and strode over to the bed. He grasped the thin wrist on the bedspread. "It's all right now, old fellow. We've licked em. You've done a fine job."

The tense face relaxed.

Mr Bagot, who had opened the door so gently that Jerry had not heard him, came into the room and bent over his patient. "Mrs Smith tells me you think he's worse. It's a good thing you had him moved here. She seems a kindly landlady. Those other lodgings he had were damp."

Jerry nodded and the apothecary looked perceptively at the sick officer.

Beneath the bandage his forehead glistened with perspiration while his glazed eyes searched their faces unseeing. Sometimes he muttered incoherently sometimes he called out loudly.

"Come here, boy! Go to Captain Ridgeway and tell him: Lieutenant Holmes's compliments and we've run out of ammunition." He turned sideways and murmured into his pillow, "Hurry, boy. Tell the captain."

"How long has he been like this?" asked Mr Bagot.

"About a quarter of an hour. I wish

to God he'd never gone to that damned sawbones in Portsmouth."

"Too late for wishing. Anyway, I don't think this recurrence is due to his clumsy handiwork. He'd have been all right if he hadn't banged his head and reopened the wound. It's infected now."

"I thought you would have returned earlier."

"So I should have done but some flashy fools tipped over the Charley's box. He was inside it. Broken wrist."

"Poor old devil! I hope you knocked the daylights out of them."

"Not precisely. I administered a couple of kicks and sent for the constable. They're cooling their heels in the roundhouse now."

"Ammunition," moaned the lieutenant. "We could capture them if we'd ammunition. Tell Captain Ridgeway — "

Jerry leant over the bed and laid a firm hand on the damp forehead. "I'm here, old man. You shall have your ammunition."

There was quietness again. The patient lay still, the clock ticked steadily; outside, a market cart rumbled past on its early journey and the porterhouse boy whistled as he collected the empty pots from doorsteps.

Mr Bagot unfastened the bandage and inspected the wound with a frown. "I've asked Mrs Smith to bring clean water. Ah! here she is."

A plump woman entered the room, carrying a bowl with a clean towel draped over it. When the doctor had completed his work he said, "He's more comfortable now. I still think he'll recover but it's a good thing you decided to visit him when you did. If you hadn't discovered his condition it might have been fatal. I'll come again in a couple of hours. I've got to see to the Charley now."

"Did he get out of his box by himself?" asked Jerry.

"No. Couldn't have managed it. He's an elderly man but there was a girl nearby who saw it all. Pretty lass. It's a blessing for the watch that she was walking the streets. She came to me at once."

"Really, Bagot," said Jerry teasingly. "I'm surprised at you. Didn't know you had a fancy for pretty young women who walk the streets. Poor Mrs Bagot!"

The apothecary gave a reluctant smile. "I'm rather worried about the girl. She's as innocent as a kitten and quite a beauty although poorly dressed in threadbare clothes."

Jerry stared down at his signet ring with a reminiscent smile. He knew a pretty girl who was as innocent as a kitten and who once wore threadbare clothes. But she was away safely tucked up in bed in his grandfather's house.

14

MRS THORNBURY was the housekeeper in an establishment on the fringes of upper-class society. Clare didn't have to sleep in a dormitory, for there were no rooms large enough in the attic storey but she shared a small, dark room overlooking the street with a kitchen maid.

Perhaps because she was so tired she could not sleep on her first night there. She sat up on the uncomfortable straw-filled mattress and felt cold shivers pass down her spine. She reached for the shawl, which she had made for her mother, and pulled it round her. It was getting thinner but it kept the draught away.

With early rising and long hours of work she got used to being very tired and enduring Mrs Thornbury's scolds.

"Look what you're doing, girl. Fancy carrying a candle at that angle! You're dropping hot wax on the carpet."

265

Clare looked down in horror. The accusation was perfectly true. She hadn't to think again of Captain Ridgeway whilst carrying a candle.

A week later she was nearly dismissed. Her instructions were to dust the books in the library. She pushed all her hair inside her mob cap, expecting that dust would fly and she glanced in the mirror over a pier table. She was thinner and paler than she had been in Dunnock Green, her skin so white that every freckle looked a dark spot by contrast. The uniform bestowed on her didn't fit very well, being too loose round the waist and hanging off her slender shoulders.

She found the library steps, which unfolded from a chair, and climbed them to reach the top books. She brought these down, a few at a time, and piled them on the floor; then rubbed the shelf and, as she had anticipated, released a mist of dust. She coughed, then began to wipe each book individually — a life of Philip II of Spain and a critical biography of Charles II by Lord Halifax. Then she discovered some books of botanical prints and one of them was written by her father. There were some illustrated books of birds and a volume about wild animals which she opened and began to read. She didn't hear the dainty ormolu clock in its glass dome strike the hour.

"Upon my word!" Mrs Thornbury's voice literally shook with anger. "Whatever are you doing? I don't hold with maids being taught their letters. What we want are strong, obedient girls, not weaklings with their noses in books. Why did you take them off the shelf?"

"But how else can I clean them?"

"With goose quills, of course! Leave the books in place and dust them as far as the wing of a goose will go. Mr Sheldon has had them all bound in brown leather with his initials in gold on the spine. If silly people take them down, they'll all get mixed up. What do you want with them, anyway?"

"My father wrote this one and did the paintings for it," said Clare quietly.

Mrs Thornbury looked disbelieving. "If I catch you reading a book again in this house, I'll send you packing and no amount of lies about your father will help you!"

She flounced out of the room, fiddling with her chatelaine to get the key for the linen cupboard.

As soon as she had a little time of her own, Clare crept upstairs and took out the workbox which had been her mother's. It was comforting to look at it.

She smoothed her fingers caressingly over the mahogany box, so well made that the brass nameplate fitted into the wood without leaving a ridge. It was the same at each end where a diminutive brass handle on the right enabled one to pull out a small drawer. For the sake of symmetry another identical handle on the left merely marked a false drawer. Clare had always thought how realistic it was and had originally been disappointed when she discovered that she couldn't pull out the drawer. Everything fitted neatly, the work of a clever craftsman. She pressed her fingers appreciatively against it and . . .

. . . the 'false' drawer flew open.

She jumped with surprise and was at first afraid that she had broken her treasure until she realised that she had merely pressed a concealed spring. She wondered if her mother had known of it, for she had never mentioned it. Clare had often seen her use the box; in fact it had been one of her mother's most prized possessions. But she must have known of the secret place because the drawer was not empty.

Inside was a folded paper, rather brown with age. It had a broken wax seal and was evidently a letter. Although the ink was faded it was easy to read the decisive handwriting which had directed it to Miss Crewe, but the letter began more familiarly, 'Dear Isabella.'

Would her mother mind if she read the letter? Clare wished she could have asked her; it must have been very private and very important to have been hidden so deliberately and kept for a lifetime. Perhaps Clare would have returned it to the drawer unread if she hadn't caught sight of the signature: Jeremiah Ridgeway. She opened it out fully and read the contents slowly.

Dear Isabella,
Since our conversation in the 'Greek Temple' was interrupted I thought I

had better communicate with you by letter. I can trust Bill Brown to bring this safely to you.

I understand that you fear your father's wrath will descend not only on you and Winster but also on his elderly parents if you elope with him now. I fully realise that this is your reason for asking me to withdraw all pretensions to your hand at the eleventh hour, so that your subsequent marriage to him will be seen in a far more favourable light from his point of view.

I want to make it clear that the only reason I was so hesitant to accede to your request was because I feel that it would be humiliating for you to appear to be publicly rejected. However, if you sincerely wish me to do this, and I can see that you do, rest assured that you need not suffer pangs of conscience on my account. I am not afraid of the damage to my reputation — I haven't got much left, anyway! If I can't suffer a little opprobrium on your behalf then my protestations of admiration for you would be meaningless — and they are not. I would have rescued you from dark towers and deep dungeons if we had lived in the days when such things were necessary. As it is, ironically I can best serve you by appearing to jilt you. I can only do this because I believe that Winster really adores you and that you reciprocate his feelings entirely. Had I been the fortunate possessor of your heart it would have been different.

So I will do what you ask tomorrow.

Forgive me for mentioning such a delicate matter but if Winster has not sufficient funds to set up his nursery garden in the way he wishes to do, I have a small legacy for which I have no particular use.

You will probably not see me again but remember I am and always shall be,

Yours to command
Jeremiah Ridgeway

Clare reread the letter which she was now holding in hands that trembled. Then a tear splashed on to it as she folded it again and replaced it safely in the concealed drawer. After that she lay face down on her narrow bed and sobbed great sobs which shook her thin body.

She cried because Jeremy Ridgeway had never gained her mother's love and, because of that, had lost his father's. Then a picture flashed into her mind. She saw Jerry again standing in the dining-room in front of the portrait of Jeremiah; she saw the expression on Jerry's face and made a firm resolution.

By some means she would show Jerry his father's letter. He must see the evidence of his parent's unselfish and chivalrous behaviour. Clare was determined that Jerry's bitter disappointment in his father would be taken away and that the character of Jeremiah Ridgeway would be vindicated.

Meanwhile, the letter had to be kept safe and she decided to replace it in the workbox. As she moved the miniature drawer something else fell forwards. It was wrapped in a soft piece of material and when she undid this she found that a small piece of paper was twisted round the hidden object. She unscrewed the paper and read the few words inscribed on it in her mother's handwriting: 'The ring Jeremiah gave me.'

A deep crimson ruby was set in the gold bezel and surrounded by diamonds which sparkled in the light. The ring was in pristine condition, possibly only worn a few times by Isabella Winster and then locked away where no one could admire the glowing jewel which Jeremiah had insisted she kept and which Isabella had hidden for twenty years.

Clare hadn't had the opportunity to see many jewels but she recognised that this ruby was larger than most. She lifted it up so that the light shone directly on it; it was impossible to study it minutely without a magnifying glass but it appeared quite flawless and she did know that very few rubies were perfect. She realised that she had a very valuable object. It was legally hers, for it had been given to her mother and was therefore Clare's by inheritance.

If she sold it she could leave her present situation. She would be freed from the fault-finding of the housekeeper and the privations of life as an overworked maid; she never need be hungry again and she could wear clothes which weren't shabby.

Yet it never occurred to her to sell it. She held it gently. This was what Jeremiah had given to Isabella and together with his letter it had to be given to his son. The proof of Jeremiah's selfless nature should go in its entirety to the Ridgeways. The immediate problem was how to get it to the captain. She wondered where he was now.

So did Lieutenant Holmes.

The lieutenant lay in bed fuming inwardly. Why was he such a cursed fool as to bang his forehead on a beam just when the wound was healing at last? He wished he had never gone into the tavern where the ceiling was so low that any man above average height must bend his head. The relapse to his health had caused also a setback in his career. The *Audax* would sail with another first lieutenant and he might find himself on half-pay, kicking his heels in the capital.

A door banged downstairs, footsteps made the stairs creak and a cheerful whistle sounded through the house.

Jerry burst open the door with a kick from his boot; his hands were full. He deposited on the table two bottles of wine, a ham, some fruit, books, a pack of cards and a backgammon board.

"Provisions aboard!" he shouted.

"Aye aye, sir," responded a voice from the bed.

"I've news for you," said Jerry. "Well, a rumour anyway. Three guesses."

"Someone's shot Boney."

"No."

"Mary Wilkins is expecting again and Jack Travers is responsible this time."

"Wrong. At least you're probably not but I haven't heard of it."

Jerry brought a chair across to the bed, turned it round, then sat astride it, leaning his arms on the back of it.

"Hurry up. Third guess."

"They're going to hang your picture of Horatio in the next Academy exhibition."

"Wrong again!" Jerry's eyes twinkled. "How would you like to be a captain?"

"It isn't possible and you might refrain from suggesting it when you know I shall be a bloody pensioner for years." The lieutenant's convalescent state made him grumpy.

"You are in the doldrums, aren't you? You can shake yourself out of them or

275

I'll do it for you literally," retorted Jerry but the merriment was still in his voice. "You've been recommended for promotion, my lad, and I reckon you'll get it."

"Are you serious?"

"Why the devil shouldn't I be? I've just come from the Admiralty."

"What happened?"

"When I explained the reasons why I cannot go to sea at present I was severely rebuked and asked where they would obtain another captain with what they called my 'dash and energy'. So I said, 'My first lieutenant is the man'. I think you'll get your ship."

"Sir!" Holmes sat upright. "You're the most complete ace!"

"Yes, I am, aren't I? They should have made more like me. One isn't enough."

"It was very quick of you. Or had you premeditated it?"

"Let's say old Greybeard played into my hands by the way he reacted."

Lieutenant Holmes frowned hurting his forehead. "Are you sure you don't want to go back to sea?"

There was no time to answer. Mrs

Smith opened the door to announce the apothecary.

Jerry retired to the window to view his latest sketch critically while Mr Bagot took his place at the bedside and removed the bandage and pronounced the wound to be healing well. Jerry decided that he had executed his drawing of Horatio's tail successfully this time; it had a small kink near the end which he had omitted on the previous sketch. This was a new picture showing the dog with his paws on Clare's apron at their first meeting. Jerry had enjoyed drawing her and found that he remembered every detail perfectly. He looked again at the picture, unaware that the apothecary had come to stand beside him. It was a very good likeness. The expression compounded of sweetness and mischief was typical of Clare, as was the slight air of vulnerability portrayed in the angle of her head and the way her hair fell forwards half-screening her cheek.

"I can't believe it!" exclaimed Mr Bagot. "It's her!"

"What?" Jerry's voice was sharp.

"This girl with the dog. She's the one who came to my house to tell me about the Charley. Of course, it can't be; you've never seen her but, if you had, you'd know what I mean."

"What the devil are you talking about?" snapped Jerry.

Mr Bagot was taken aback. This wasn't the jovial captain he thought he understood. He suddenly remembered his position as a humble apothecary and that it was the captain who would pay his bill. He said contritely, "I beg your pardon. YOU can't know this girl; she's come from Yorkshire to London, seeking a position as a domestic servant. The child's an orphan."

"My God! Where did you say she had come from?"

"Yorkshire. I don't know exactly where."

"What colour are her eyes?"

"Green."

"Green?" Jerry was pouring ale from an earthenware jug into a tankard. "Green, did you say?" He put down the jug, spilling ale on the table.

"That's right. She's a pretty girl with that pale skin inclined to freckles."

"How many?"

"I beg your pardon! I did not count her freckles, sir."

Jerry chuckled. "Of course not. I did," he added softly to himself. "What's her name?"

"I don't know."

"Good God! The girl was in distress and you didn't even trouble to discover who she was!"

Lieutenant Holmes felt some sympathy for the apothecary. Jerry Ridgeway was the kindest, most amiable man in the world ninety per cent of the time but the other ten per cent he was like the point of a rapier — steely and sharp. It was an unlucky man who was the wrong end of that cutting blade.

Mr Bagot laid a hand on the back of a chair and wished he could sit down, but he maintained a quiet dignity. "I did not ask her name. She seemed reticent to reveal anything about herself, but I gathered that she was destitute."

"Destitute! Who the hell do you think you are? A man devoted to healing or a complacent ninnyhammer allowing an unprotected girl to roam the streets alone without even ascertaining who she was?

Now I suppose we've to scout every rookery in London to find out who's kidnapped her and all because of a damned sawbones with no more brains than a louse!"

Mr Bagot gripped the back of the chair tightly and tried to avoid those angry black eyes but he contrived to answer calmly, "I did manage to acquire a respectable situation for her, sir."

The captain cursed himself. "I'm sorry, Bagot. I'm raging at you when I'm the one to blame. I never should have left Yorkshire."

"I understood she had no relations, sir."

"If it's Clare, she has — one, a grandfather and he's lucky to be over two hundred miles away. I should have dealt with him before even if he is twice my age. The more fool me for being so merciful!"

He poured some ale into a tankard and handed it to the doctor. "Drink that and forgive me."

Mr Bagot succumbed to the disarming smile. He described every detail concerning Clare that he could remember and his listener was totally convinced of her identity. "Can you furnish me with her direction?"

"Easily." He took a notebook from his pocket and scribbled the address on a page, then tore it out and gave it to Jerry.

When the apothecary had gone, Jerry wrenched open the door of the clothes press. He tossed a clean shirt on to the bed and announced that he was hot. "I'd better have a good wash before I go."

"Don't forget your sword," recommended Holmes.

"Sword? If anyone interferes with Clare, it's my fist they'll feel. I keep my sword for gentlemen."

"I didn't mean that. I thought you were getting ready to go to Carlton House."

"Carlton House?" Jerry uttered an obscene oath. "I'd forgotten that. Well, I can't go now. I'm off to fetch Clare."

"You can't fail to turn up at Carlton House!" exclaimed Holmes, forgetting that he was speaking to a superior officer. "It's nearly treason! You accepted the invitation. Anyway, it was a command really. You're the apple of Prinny's eye since you told him about Trafalgar."

"Damn his eyes!"

Holmes sighed. His head ached and it was never easy to argue with Jerry. People said he got his stubbornness from his grandfather. Heaven protect anyone who offended them both at the same time! He persisted patiently: "I understand that the Regent wants them to give you a KCB."

"What the hell do I care about that?"

"Nothing. But, if I read the signs correctly, it would enable this Clare to become Lady Ridgeway."

Jerry stood quite still staring through the window. "Yes, I suppose so. She would never seek a title but she deserves one."

He threw his boots into the corner.

"Relax," said Lieutenant Holmes.

Jerry gave a crack of laughter. "You insubordinate rascal! I shall wait until you're better and then I'll give you such a drubbing you'll need Bagot again!"

★ ★ ★

Mrs Sheldon gave a small dinner party and the butler complained that he

282

hadn't enough footmen to wait at table; so Mrs Thornbury suggested that Clare should serve in the dining-room. She was standing unobtrusively by the sideboard when the first guests entered the room. A strident voice interrupted the others and Clare recognised Lady Corton, who had dismissed her when his lordship had embraced Clare on the half-landing. Probably the lady would not recognise her but would the husband?

Clare bent her head over the pile of plates she was holding and tried to hide her face so that his lordship wouldn't recall her but the butler ordered her to pass something to a guest on Lord Corton's right. Despite her silent, unobtrusive movements he noticed her and made a fumbling motion towards her hips with his big hand. She whisked herself away and he called her back to ask for an extra and unnecessary plate. Clare had the utmost longing to hurl a bowl of white soup in his face.

Back in her position by the sideboard she became aware of his lecherous scrutiny. She glanced towards the butler, hoping he wouldn't send her back to serve on that side of the table. When something was required from the kitchen she volunteered to fetch it and didn't wait to be told that she was supposed to stay in the dining room.

She was deeply thankful when the ladies withdrew and the servants left the gentlemen to privacy and port.

Later, when she was told to help clear the dining-room, she realised how much they had consumed. The table was littered with glasses; one of those near Lord Corton's chair was broken; its stem containing spirals of coloured glass was snapped in two. There was a damask napkin with a dark red stain on it; every decanter was empty and a chair had been overturned. Someone had scored a mark on the polished table with the prong of a fork. No one had troubled to snuff the candles and grease had congealed on the silver candelabrum.

The air was putrid with the fumes of brandy and the smoke of cigars. Mary, who was helping Clare to clear the room, wrinkled her nose and expressed herself forcefully, "Gawd! The place don't 'alf stink!"

Clare filled a tray with empty glasses which she carried to the kitchen where the young footman was in trouble with the butler, who was so absorbed in berating his junior that Clare was given the task of taking the tea tray to the drawing-room. She didn't return to the dining-room.

So she wasn't present when Mary, offended by the atmosphere, flung open a sash window and then absentmindedly placed a branch of burning candles on the pier table beside it. She gathered up more glasses and carried them on a heavy silver tray. She hadn't a free hand, so she left the door wide open.

No one was there to see that a gust of wind had blown the striped curtain sideways, where it caught the guttering candles and began to burn.

15

JERRY descended the grand staircase at Carlton House, smiling in mild amazement at the elegance around him. He wore full-dress uniform of dark blue cloth coat with stand-fall collar and square lapels trimmed with gold lace, the two gold epaulettes and the double row of gold lace on his cuffs proclaiming his rank and seniority. His waistcoat, breeches and stockings were of pristine whiteness and a sword, suspended from a black sword belt, hung at his side. As he reached the hall a flunkey in the royal livery stepped forward.

"Captain Ridgeway?"

"Yes."

The man proffered a silver salver with a letter resting on it.

"I am informed, sir, that this has been sent here from your lodgings because it was thought that it might be urgent."

"Thank you."

Jerry took it, broke the seal and was

surprised to find that it was from Mr Bagot, the apothecary. He stood under the glass skylight, reading it, with his head bent over the epistle and his hand resting on the hilt of his sword which he suddenly gripped tightly. "My God!" he exclaimed and strode decisively across the chequered tiles, frowning at the classical urns and busts arranged in a recess above the pillars.

He almost ran between the Corinthian columns of the portico to hail a hackney and, having given the address of Mr Sheldon's house, instructed the driver to go there quickly.

"Can't do that, I'm afraid, sir. There's a house there on fire. Dreadful blaze it is. I dare say there'll be folks come to gape at it, but they're fools. I've seen fires like that before now. You never know when a burning timber will fall on your 'ead. No, sir, I ain't going along 'ay Hill."

★ ★ ★

Mr Sheldon was harassed. His head was clearing now from the effects of after-dinner drinking but he felt a long way

287

from everything, even from the burning building which was his home. There was an air of unreality about everything. It couldn't be true that his house was on fire; he felt that he would soon awake from his nightmare. He was so stunned that it didn't occur to him to send a message to the insurance company whose metal plate was fixed to the wall. The wooden shutters were burning and his butler had suggested ripping them away from the wall but Mr Sheldon refused to allow this because whoever tried it might get hurt.

Clare broke into a sudden perspiration which was not due to the heat of the fire. She had left her best possession indoors. When Mary had called upstairs to warn her of the outbreak of fire she had rushed to warn another maid and thought of nothing else. Now she looked up frantically at the house. Right at the top of it was her mother's workbox and, much more important, inside it was the letter which proved beyond doubt the unselfish behaviour of Jeremiah Ridgeway. It was the epistle which could bring so much relief to Jerry.

She had to get it while there was still time.

Mary, sick with fright, was clinging to her arm. "Look after her!" Clare shouted to the footman, pressing the girl's hand into his and then she fled across the road.

Smoke billowed round the door and Clare paused, coughing, suddenly frightened for her life. She might die in that torrid, crackling house. "Come back!" shrieked a voice from the crowd and someone ran forward to restrain her. It was that which decided her and it was amazing how much she was able to think in only a second or two. If anyone tried to pull her back, they would succeed, for they would almost certainly be stronger than she was. Then she would be unable to get the letter for Jerry and he needed it to have his father's true nature proved beyond doubt. Accepting the risk to herself she ran through the open door before anyone could stop her.

She had to reach that workbox and if she dashed up the backstairs, she would just have time to get it.

She didn't feel afraid as she ran up

289

the stairs, only excited to think that she was going to get the vital document. Her heart was beating rapidly and she ran up those stairs quicker than she had ever moved before.

She entered her bedchamber, knelt beside the bed and lifted out the box. She could hear a roaring sound from the direction of the stairs and realised that it might be very difficult to get out quickly. It would be better not to be encumbered, so she decided to abandon the box itself and simply take the letter and ring. Accordingly, she placed the box on the bed and felt along the little drawer. By now a pulse was beating in her neck and her head was banging. She was fighting a temptation to panic and realised that she was pressing the right-hand drawer instead of the left one; she began to press that and was just wondering whether she had better take the whole box because the spring wasn't going to work when it shot open and she extracted the precious letter which she put securely inside the bodice of her gown so that she could keep both hands free. She slid the ring on to the centre finger of her right hand.

It was a little too big but it ought to be safe.

Meanwhile, a gust of wind had blown through the front door which she had left open. This fed the fire and a tongue of flame spread to the elegant curved staircase and licked at the banister. In the draught it did not take long for the fire to leap up the staircase well.

In the street outside flames flickered against the darkness. A cloud of smoke blew over the watchers, causing many to cough while the lambent orange crackled around the door. A sudden burst of flame from a window caused a scream of terror from the crowd, while the reflection of the firelight lit up the surrounding buildings.

The orange flames were in constant motion, rising higher in sudden bursts and a yellow flame began to lick another window frame on the ground floor while Mary coughed so much she was nearly sick. The ground-floor room filled with a lurid red light against which the bars of the window appeared gaunt and black. A gust of black smoke billowed out thickly, the wind fanned the flames and the smoke whirled round in spirals.

Someone shouted, "There's a woman in there!"

Mr Sheldon started forward in a frantic movement and two men simultaneously grabbed his arms and pulled him back. "It's no good, sir. There's nothing you can do."

"William, don't leave me!" screamed his wife.

At that cry he ceased fighting for the freedom to rush headlong into an inferno. Instead he buried his face in his hands unable to look.

Someone brought one of the parish ladders which had been designed to reach a third storey but decided it was useless and simply laid it beside the railings before retreating to greater safety on the opposite side of the road.

Two men rushed up bearing a couple offhand squirts, part of the parish fire-fighting equipment. "It's a bit late for them," shouted someone.

It was. The men trying to operate them were driven back by the heat near the door.

"Look at the fire mark quickly!" called

another voice and a woman pointed at the metal plate near Mr Sheldon's front door. "The company must be informed."

"Aye, that's right. They'll send an engine."

"Oh, God!" shrieked one of the crowd. "There's that girl, look! At the window there!"

Even now Clare didn't really believe she was going to die. She looked to right and left again, still expecting that somewhere there was an escape route. She had no sense of foreboding, just the feeling that something very frightening was happening but that soon she would have found the way out. Escape had to be possible.

She was extremely hot. Behind her the door of the room crashed and a hot surge of flame engulfed that exit. The scorching fire was coming nearer and it was so hard to breathe.

She pushed her head through the window, forcing the sash up further and so unwittingly fanned the flames. Then she looked down and saw that already a tongue of orange licked the blackened and charred windowframe on the ground floor. If she stood on the window ledge and jumped she would get caught in that flame.

There was no way she could go.

She accepted it then — the inevitability of death. She was going to die. She really was. In a few minutes. Amazingly she felt perfectly calm. She could almost hear her mother's words, 'Death is only like opening the door to another room'. Her mother had died confidently.

Jerry would be brave if it were he . . .

She leaned forward, again conscious of the intensity of the heat behind her. She didn't fear death but she feared those flames. She shut her eyes.

The bystanders shouted with terror as the conflagration increased. The dark silhouette of a man in naval uniform was etched against the bright background of the flames.

"Don't stand so close!" shouted an Irish chairman who had left his sedan chair at the end of the street with his partner and hurried up to stand transfixed with awe at the sight.

"You there! Hold this!" commanded the naval officer, unbuckling his sword belt. He then thrust the black sword belt and his weapon into the Irishman's hands and seized the abandoned ladder, which he lifted into position against the house to the left of the burning fabric, balancing it as carefully as possible. Seconds later he was on his way up it while the crowd gasped and exclaimed to one another, craning their necks to see the figure which was just visible as the smoke whirled around him.

"How brave he is!"

"The man's suicidal. He can't hope to get her safely down."

"What courage!"

"I can't bear to look!"

"I can only just see the girl."

Clare still stood with her hands on the window-sill and her eyes shut. She wanted to cry out but she couldn't. Her breath was coming in little, short gasps and she felt very sick. She was going to faint.

"Don't faint; don't fall backwards. Don't faint; don't fall backwards."

Something seemed to be urging her not to give way as though, if only she could stand a moment longer, she would be safe, would get out of here. But how could she?

Hardly able to think, she stood utterly motionless.

"Don't faint; don't fall backwards!" It sounded like a real human voice, like Jerry's.

"Put your hands on my shoulders. Clare! Put your hands on my shoulders!"

Clare was so dazed she couldn't believe he was really there and she stayed immobile, although she opened her eyes and Jerry's face swam before her gaze.

"Put your hands on my shoulders, Clare! At once!" It was his quarterdeck voice and she obeyed the command immediately.

She was lifted over the ledge and laid across Jerry's shoulder. His authoritative voice had dispelled the sense of unreality. It was truly Jerry and she wasn't imprisoned in that room any longer. For a moment she almost dared to expect to get to safety and then fear returned as one of the timbers fell with a crash inside the house, someone in the crowd below screamed and an extra surge of flame intensified the heat and brightness. Suppose the ladder caught fire! Then Jerry would perish too — a horrific possibility.

Conscious of her billowing skirts and the danger that they would catch alight, she kept one arm round Jerry's neck but used her other hand to hold her flowing gown as close to her side as she could do, which helped Jerry, for the thin material had already blown across his face once, hiding his view of the ladder rungs.

Everything seemed to spin round as Clare lay with her head downwards. They were level with the worst of the fire now.

"Hold tight!" shouted Jerry.

Hardly able to hope or fear any longer she could only pray wordlessly.

"He'll never do it!" called an agitated voice.

Then the roar of the flames grew greater.

"They'll both be burnt to death!" screamed someone.

Suddenly they weren't moving downwards any more. Jerry was carrying her across the street. There was a cheer from the onlookers, but neither the captain nor the girl he bore heard it.

"It's unbelievable!" A man exclaimed. "Well done, sir!"

Jerry didn't reply. He just coughed and coughed while the sweat ran down his face and neck.

Two men, who had climbed to the attic storey of the houses opposite to the Sheldons', were trying rather unsuccessfully to douse the flames by directing streams of water from the hand squirts.

Clare, having been set on her feet, stood rather unsteadily, leaning against Jerry. She swayed and felt blackness closing round her. Instantly he lifted her up again and held her in his arms.

The parish constable was trying to organise the other householders, getting them to pass leather buckets of water down the street from hand to hand.

"That's useless," complained a man in a frieze coat. "It's too late to stop it spreading further unless they bring gunpowder and blow up the house next door."

Despite the crackling of the flames,

pounding hooves could be heard. The sound came nearer with the rumble of wheels.

"The engine! Thank God the engine's here!"

Drawn by grey horses and driven with urgency, the company's fire engine approached at speed with the red-coated fire-fighters clinging to it and shouting from beneath their tall hats to warn bystanders to get out of the way quickly.

Now the constable ordered the helpers to put down the parish fire buckets and come to assist at the company's engine instead. Persons were needed to help in pumping so that sufficient water would be sucked up the leather hose.

Although a number of onlookers went willingly to help at the pumps, even more surrounded Jerry, looking at him with incredulity. They simply hadn't expected to see him alive and standing beside them again.

"By all the saints! Oi've nivver seen anything like it," exclaimed the Irishman. "Your sword, sir."

"What?" asked Jerry vaguely. "Oh, yes;

follow behind with it, will you?"

"And count it an honour, sir; only thankful your excellency wasn't roasted alive. Oi've nivver seen the like. Sure I wouldn't have believed it possible."

Jerry's face was ashen and streaked with soot and there was a livid red mark on the back of his hand. Suddenly there was nothing else anyone could say and they drew back into the shadows.

The captain walked down the street with hasty strides, carrying his burden to the hackney just parked at the end. The jarvey, who had earned a sovereign by obeying the command to wait there for Jerry, exclaimed in horror at what he saw. He opened the door and Jerry stumbled inside, placed Clare on the seat and received his sword from the Irishman, whom he rewarded before the door was shut.

The floor of the vehicle was covered in dirty straw and the seat was shabby but Jerry sank back on to it thankfully, closed his eyes and tried not to feel the pain in his hand.

For a few minutes Clare lay back against the dilapidated upholstery, enduring waves of faintness and nausea. All the time she was vaguely conscious that there was something she had to do. As the weak, sick feeling abated she opened her eyes and looked at the dark shape of the man beside her and felt the jogging motion of the vehicle. The roar of flames had died away and the most persistent sound was the clopping of hooves and the rumble of wheels along the cobbles.

"Captain Ridgeway, I suppose I sound stupid but it really is you, isn't it?"

A weary laugh answered her. "Of course it is — all twelve stone of me."

The light from the lamp suddenly flashed on the ring she wore so that diamonds shimmered round the ruby. She slipped it off her finger. "You should have this," she said but her voice was husky and Jerry didn't hear. He was gritting his teeth as he tried to ignore the searing pain in his hand.

"Captain Ridgeway." Clare tried to enunciate the words but her voice was just a croak.

"Don't try to speak until you've had a drink."

But she had to give it to him; so

she raised the braided flap on his coat and placed the ruby ring in his pocket, pushing it into the corner so that it would be secure.

"Captain Ridgeway."

"Yes." He was gritting his teeth again and the beads of perspiration stood on his forehead visible in the lamplight.

"I want you to have the letter."

"What letter?" He turned his head against the squabs to look at her.

"The one I went back for."

"Where is it?"

"In the bodice of my gown."

"Is that an invitation?"

Clare giggled weakly. She put her hand into the bodice of her high-waisted gown and pulled out the letter, explaining as she did so, "I didn't dare drop it in case it fell into the flames. Read it later. It's from your father."

Naturally, he thought she was confused due to her appalling experience. She couldn't be giving him a letter from his father; but he put out his hand to take it and she saw the livid scar across the back of it.

"Jerry! Your hand!"

He withdrew it hastily and substituted the other. "It's just a scorch mark I got as I came past the downstairs window."

"It must be agony! How dreadful for you!" Her self-control broke at the sight of Jerry's painful hand and she burst into tears.

"Why, sweetheart! It's not worth tears."

He put the letter unread into his pocket and pulled Clare close to him. The gold lace on his uniform scratched her cheek but its nearness was comforting. He kissed her soft hair, then laid his cheek against it. Several times she tried to thank him for his courage in rescuing her but he merely repeated his adjuration to her not to talk until she had been given a drink.

When they reached his lodgings Jerry paid the jarvey and helped Clare out of the hackney. He surveyed her smoke-blackened gown and dirty face before glancing down at his white breeches stained with soot. He made a grimace, "I only require a brush over my shoulder to be taken for a sweep."

"What I must look like I can't

imagine," she replied. She was sufficiently recovered from the shock of her ordeal to feel self-conscious.

He wiped a smut from her cheek. "You look as pretty as ever but not nearly as clean!"

"Are these your lodgings?"

"Yes. I lodged here when I was a penniless lieutenant without a ship. So, when I discovered poor Holmes, who had been with me on the *Audax*, in a very uncomfortable room I brought him here."

He ushered Clare into the small, narrow hall and said, "It may not be good for your reputation to stay with two bachelors but Mrs Smith can help to care for you."

There was an oil-lamp burning on a small table in the hall and Lieutenant Holmes appeared in a nightshirt at the top of the stairs, carrying another lamp. He affected to stifle a yawn and survey the clock before he spoke in a teasing tone. "So you've decided to come home! Eight bells and still out! I suppose you've been at a royal orgy!"

"Not quite," answered Jerry in a voice

of forced cheerfulness but he leaned against the wall.

The lieutenant didn't notice. He descended the stairs still joking. "Real tomcat on the tiles, eh? Been on the prowl and — my God! what's happened?"

He was close to Jerry now and the light from both lamps illuminated the captain's face.

It was ashy grey with a black smear down the left cheek. His hair, which was slightly scorched, fell forward across his forehead and when he tried to push it back, Holmes saw the long, red scar across his hand. There were rusty burns along his sleeve, which was torn, but he drew Clare forward. "This is Miss Winster and she needs looking after."

"So do you!"

"Nonsense!" retorted Jerry sharply.

Holmes ignored the riposte. "Mrs Smith!" he shouted. "Mrs Smith, come here quickly!" Jerry had just swayed.

The captain stood upright again with determination and gave the lieutenant a playful cuff over the ear. "Don't frighten the poor woman. There's nothing wrong with me."

Mrs Smith came on to the landing, clutching a shawl round her plump shoulders.

"Are you ill, Mr Holmes? Is it housebreakers? If only Captain Ridgeway were here! Dear me, I jumped straight out of bed and now I feel quite faint."

She came heavily downstairs. "So, it's not housebreakers! It's the captain himself." She came nearer and gasped. "Oh, sir! You almost look as if you'd been in a fire."

"Surely not!" quipped Jerry. "I've just fallen in the river."

Clare giggled as he wanted her to do but Mrs Smith, who had a very prosaic mind, shook her head and remarked in a puzzled voice, "I should have thought that your coat would have been wet."

"For God's sake, get him some brandy!" snapped Holmes.

"Yes sir, directly. The poor young lady looks as if she's in trouble, too."

"Well, get her some as well."

"What we really require is soap and water," explained Jerry. He led Clare upstairs, calling to Mrs Smith to fill a hip-bath with warm water.

Mrs Smith was a motherly individual and she was soon exclaiming over Clare's condition while helping her to undress. Immersed from the waist down in warm water, Clare asked to be allowed to wash her hair.

"You look too tired to bother."

"But I can't bear it like this," protested Clare. "It smells of smoke." She was dazed but there was something soothing about scented soap and warm water.

Mrs Smith washed her hair and dried it on a warm towel, praising its copper glints, while in the next room Mallow divested the captain of his clothes and assisted him to bathe and don a clean shirt and pantaloons. He advised Jerry to retire for what little was left of the night, but he refused. He offered one concession — he would wear his dressing-gown instead of a coat. Then he strolled into the little apartment which did duty as a drawing-room.

Clare borrowed a bedgown from Mrs Smith and while she adjusted the frilled cuffs she thought about Jerry. As the shock of her experience wore off she became very curious to know how he could have arrived so opportunely. It seemed incredible. She was so eager to discover the truth that without a thought for the impropriety of her action she put down the hairbrush, thanked her hostess and ran into the room where the men were talking.

Jerry caught his breath as he saw her framed in the doorway with her hair released over her slender shoulders. She was quite inadequately clothed and the borrowed garment was too long for her. She caught her toe in the hem and fell headlong into Lieutenant Holmes's arms.

"Just what I've always wanted!" he exclaimed. "But I have a feeling the captain has a prior claim."

Jerry laughed. "Exactly. Unhand the lady at once, you scoundrel!"

"Aye aye, sir!"

The lieutenant released Clare with a chuckle and Jerry caught her round the waist. He looked down at her. "You ought to be in bed — a thought which fills me with temptation. Holmes, get my boat cloak quickly."

His request was obeyed rapidly and

Jerry placed the heavy blue cloak over her shoulders. She put her hands behind her head and lifted her hair out of the stand-fall collar before he fastened it at the neck with the small chain looped between two brass lion's-head clasps.

"What's puzzling you, Green Eyes?" He pinched her cheek gently.

"How could you have arrived so opportunely? It seemed an incredible coincidence and I can't thank you enough."

"It wasn't a coincidence. It was due to Bagot."

"Bagot?"

"The sawbones who's been attending Holmes here." He explained how the apothecary had recognised her from a sketch. "I was going to come round tomorrow and remove you from Mr Sheldon's home. Your proper place is in Dunnock Green, my girl. But Bagot saw the fire when he was on his way to visit a patient. He sent an urgent message to me at Carlton House. Naturally, he didn't know that you were in danger but he thought you would become homeless and that I should want to know. I jumped into a hackney at once and you know the rest."

Again she tried to thank him but he shook his head and led her to a seat. "We might as well have some supper or breakfast or whatever one calls it at this hour and then you can go to sleep."

She was so tired that she could hardly eat the chicken brought to her and marvelled at the quantity of cold beef which Jerry consumed. She looked pale and the shadows under her eyes emphasised her ordeal and lack of sleep, but she was now fresh and clean; her cheeks appeared positively scrubbed and a faint odour of country herbs clung to her person.

Market carts were beginning to rumble through the streets and dawn had lightened the sky before she climbed into Mrs Smith's second-best bed and pulled up the quilt.

16

CLARE slept late next morning. She didn't hear Jerry shouting to Mallow, demanding his razor and shaving water. She was still deeply asleep while he ate breakfast with the lieutenant.

"What's worrying you, Holmes?"

"I wonder what kind of captain I'll be. I'm not like you. I'll wager every man on board will loathe me within a week."

"Nonsense! You've got courage. You'll seek out the enemy and destroy him, which is what the men want. Bravery and prize money are — What the devil's that noise? Sounds like one of Mr Watt's steam engines."

"Do they swear? Because someone outside is cursing eloquently."

"Open the door, woman!" came a gruff voice. "Don't stand there gawping. I want to go in and sit down."

"Yes, sir. I beg your pardon, sir." Mrs Smith turned the door knob.

Jerry looked up. "My God! It's the old gentleman!"

Mr Ridgeway was leaning on his ebony cane while he regained his breath. "Yes, it is and you might be more welcoming. I want a chair and a drink."

"Of course." Jerry hurried forward. "I never thought you'd come to town again, sir."

"Neither did I. I dare swear it'll kill me. Noisy, dirty, expensive place."

"Is there a particular reason for your visit?"

"Of course there is. You don't think I wanted to come, do you?"

Jerry grimaced. "For one egotistical moment I thought you wanted to see me."

"Well, I don't. I think you're going to be angry when you hear what I've got to tell you." He directed a reproving stare at Holmes, who looked acutely embarrassed. He was going to leave the Ridgeways alone but he wished he had done so a moment earlier instead of receiving that penetrating look. The old man had an eye like a gimlet. With a mumbled apology Holmes went out of the room.

Mr Ridgeway lowered himself ponderously into a chair, complaining, "I can't imagine why you live up two pairs of stairs. What's wrong with the first floor?"

"These are my quarters."

"They're damned inconvenient. You should stay at a proper hotel, like I am doing. Climbing up here leaves a fellow gasping. It's like roosting with the pigeons on St Paul's. And who the devil's the chap wandering around in a nightgown?"

"That's Holmes, my first lieutenant. He was wounded when we had that encounter with the *Joyeux*."

"He was, eh? I suppose if a fox came in here to hide from hounds you'd shelter it."

"I expect I should," agreed Jerry imperturbably.

"I'm thirsty," announced his grandfather.

"I'll ask Mrs Smith to make you some tea."

"That's not what I meant. I didn't climb up here for a basinful of pap."

Jerry grinned, poured a glass of Madeira and handed it to his grandfather.

Looking down at him he asked, "Why did you come, sir?"

"You'll be in a rage when I tell you so sit down. I don't want you towering over me."

Jerry laughed, sat down, plunged his hands in the pockets of his breeches and stretched his booted legs across the hearthrug.

"She's gone," said Mr Ridgeway laconically.

"Who?"

"Clare." The old man's voice was gruffer than usual as he sought to cover up his anxiety. "Her grandfather wrote some stupid scrawl telling her she was a nuisance to us and she believed him. I've known for years that Crewe was an outsider."

"And you came here to tell me? All the way to London?"

"Yes; I'm an old fool but I thought you'd want to find the silly chit and you might need help. I could see you'd fallen for the girl. I wasn't born yesterday."

"No, indeed!"

"Don't stare at me with the same cheeky expression you had when you were twelve. You've not improved with keeping, Jeremy Ridgeway. You can give me another glass of wine and don't look as if you were an old maiden aunt wondering if I really need it."

Jerry laughed and poured him some more Madeira. "So you decided I was in love with Clare. You were right but I hadn't known it was so obvious."

"It was like looking in a mirror. You're one of those damned fools who can only be satisfied with one particular woman. I was like that, God help me."

Jerry dropped a hand on the bowed shoulder. "It's better that way. But I'm grateful for your trouble and I've found Clare."

Mr Ridgeway slopped some wine on to his knee, swore and began ineffectually to mop it up. "Where were you when you found her?"

"On the top of a ladder."

Mr Ridgeway snorted. "If you're in one of those moods when you can't take anything seriously, I may as well go. And let me tell you, you're looking very untidy. I thought you'd brought Mallow with you. What have you done to your hair? It looks burnt."

"Clare and I got a bit mixed up in a fire."

The old man's eyebrows drew together and he barked anxiously, "What?"

"Nothing to worry about. Her employer's house caught fire and I happened to arrive soon after."

"You mean you climbed up and got her?"

Jerry nodded. "She's quite all right."

"Thank God I didn't know anything about it! Silly fools, both of you! Why can't you stay where it's safe?"

Jerry grinned and gave him a brief résumé of what had happened. Mr Ridgeway nodded approval. "You acted very speedily." He got up and walked stiffly. "Suppose I might as well go to my club whilst I'm here. Haven't been for years. Wonder if old Hatchet-Face will be there. No, I don't think he could be; he must be close on eighty. I might see Mungo, but he had a scapegrace of a grandson so he's probably in his grave now. I wonder if there's anyone left of my set."

His voice sounded plaintive and Jerry said quickly, "Come back here for a nuncheon. We're your set now."

"That's right." The old man straightened his shoulders. "Try not to do anything dam' silly whilst I'm away."

"I'll make no promises I can't keep," retorted Jerry.

Two hours later Clare appeared in a borrowed gown intended for Mrs Smith's married daughter.

"Better now, Green Eyes?"

"Very much, thank you. I've been wondering however you climbed so high so quickly. The last time I had looked down there wasn't even a ladder."

"Ah! But I'd climbed the church steeple, not to mention punishments up the mainmast and journeys up and down the rigging! Clare, why did you go back into the house?"

"I thought I told you last night."

"Did you? I'm sorry."

"It's no wonder you don't remember; you must have been in considerable pain at the time. In the hackney carriage I gave you a letter from your father. The reason I went into the house was to fetch it. I think you put it in your coat pocket."

He pulled the bell-rope and demanded his uniform. Mrs Smith returned with a message from Mallow that he had sponged the coat but it wasn't fit to wear. Jerry said he had no intention of wearing the damned thing but Mallow was to send it down at once.

Mallow came hastily with the coat. Jerry laid it on the table, knocking the polished top with the gilded epaulette while he felt in the pocket with his unbandaged hand. He was rather clumsy so Clare held the coat still while he found the folded paper. He gave her a friendly grin and tried to open it, which was difficult when one hand was swathed in strips of white linen.

"Curse this bandage! I'll have it off soon or I shan't be able to ride."

"I only discovered the letter a few days ago but I couldn't let it be burnt when you hadn't read it."

"You risked your life to get this last night and I never even read it! Good God!"

He succeeded in opening it and gave a

start of surprise when he saw his father's characteristic signature. Strange how the handwriting of someone you loved was so evocative of their personality that after their death you could never view it unmoved. He walked deliberately over to the window and stood with his back to the room while he read what his parent had written over thirty years ago to Isabella Winster.

He remained standing very erect while Clare locked and unlocked her fingers, wondering if she ought to slip unobtrusively out of the room. He stood gazing out of the window; his firm, tall figure silhouetted against the light. "Poor Papa!"

Clare, feeling her presence must be an intrusion, went quietly towards the door.

"Where are you going?" He swung round.

"I thought you might prefer to be alone."

"Come back! I can't tell you what it means to me to read this but you shouldn't have risked your life to get it. Don't you understand? You are far more important to me than anything."

She began to talk quickly to hide her shyness. "If my mother had made your father happy, as he deserved, Mr Ridgeway wouldn't have been so harsh to you. I'm sorry."

"It's well worth a few beatings from my grandfather. If your mama had accepted my father it would have been pretty awkward for me now."

She looked puzzled.

He came to stand beside her. "Brothers can't marry sisters, Clare; it isn't allowed!"

He was very close now. She was vividly conscious of the determined chin above the white neckcloth and the broad shoulder and muscular body. She could so easily succumb to him. With an effort that was physical she drew back. "No! I haven't got to marry you. I should be an embarrassment. Everyone would make you feel uncomfortable because I'm only a servant."

"What damned nonsense! I shouldn't care if you were but everyone knows you're Crewe's granddaughter!"

Her grandfather had been right. He was very persuasive and for his sake she hadn't to listen. A tear ran down her cheek.

Jerry bent over her. "What's the matter, my sweet?"

If she didn't go rapidly he would overcome her scruples and that wasn't fair to him. She spoke quickly. "It's no good, Jerry, I can't do it. I won't marry you." A feeling of hopelessness engulfed her, for she had to go away from him now for ever. Jerry looked at her; she was very determined, this undernourished girl.

Neither of them had heard Mr Ridgeway arrive and they jumped when his voice boomed from the open door. "What's the matter with you, minx? Isn't my grandson good enough for you?"

Jerry ignored him. "I know I'm not much of a catch. I understand now how my father felt when your mother wouldn't have him but I shan't do as he did and marry someone else. It's a mistake."

"But they produced you!"

"Now I wish they hadn't."

"Oh, Jerry!" Tears rolled down Clare's cheeks.

The captain drew her into his arms and rocked her gently to and fro. "I'm sorry. I shouldn't have said that. It wasn't fair."

"God Almighty grant me patience!" besought Mr Ridgeway. "You're a damned, stupid, obstinate pair. If you weren't bigger than I am I'd give you a good thrashing, Jerry, like I used to do. As for this silly wench — "

"Don't speak of her like that!"

Clare tried to explain. "I can't marry him, sir, because I should be an encumbrance. He is a very kind person and I mustn't take advantage of that. It would be an imposition for me, a maid, to accept his proposal."

"Crewe has done his work well, hasn't he?" said Mr Ridgeway scathingly.

"What do you mean?" Jerry rapped out the question.

"I've interviewed Mrs Panton and spoken to Crewe. It was easy to work out what happened. He's been telling her to get out of your life or she'll ruin it."

"Clare, is this true?"

She glanced up through her lashes and saw Jerry's dark eyes. He was so near but in a few minutes she would be outside searching for domestic work and she would never see him again.

"My grandfather is right, Jerry. It would be humiliating for you if — "

"Nonsense!" Jerry shook her slightly. "Would you have married me if he hadn't written to you?"

She hesitated. It was so difficult to lie to him.

"You would! Well, you will do! I'm not giving you any choice, my girl. You WILL marry me."

"That's right, Jerry," approved Mr Ridgeway. "Take a firm line. You should have done so before instead of all that sloppy cuddling." He pinched Clare's cheek. "I'm sorry to say this about your only relative but I wanted to put a bullet through him when I learnt he'd sent you away." He held out a hand which shook slightly. "The trouble is I'm not so steady as I used to be but I think I could still do it."

"Please don't!"

"It's all right, my dear." He gave a deep chuckle. "I heaped coals of fire on him instead — told him we should make restitution for what Jeremiah did to

Isabella. I said Jerry would marry you."

"You cunning old devil!" Jerry gave a crack of laughter. "Did he believe you?"

"He believed you would marry her but I think he knows it's for love. He is pretending to believe the reason I gave because it soothes his pride. You needn't worry, Clare; he'll make certain you will be well received in society for his own sake. In any case he daren't slight Jerry's wife. He's frightened of Jerry. Don't wonder. My grandson's a fiery young whelp. Can you bear to marry him?"

"If I shan't injure him in society."

"Course you won't!"

Jerry put up a hand. "Allow me to make my own proposal. Miss Winster, will you do me the honour of accepting my hand in marriage?"

Could the daring captain really wish to marry a penniless girl whose only relative didn't want her? Clare looked up, saw the expression in his dark eyes and knew that he could. She raised her face and felt quite breathless with excitement as Jerry bent towards her. His dark head swam before her eyes and as he pressed her body close to his they both forgot Mr Ridgeway. He watched them exchange a long, passionate kiss before he exclaimed, "You certainly look like Jeremiah and Isabella."

"But we're not exactly like they were," said Jerry, raising his head. "I'll tell you something about them one day but not now."

There was a discreet knock at the door and Mallow brought Jerry's scorched uniform back into the room. "I found this in the pocket, sir."

The captain strode across the floor and took the small object, then exclaimed in surprise at what he held. Mr Ridgeway came to look. In the palm of Jerry's hand was the ruby ring. A circle of diamonds shimmered like winter frost round the rose-red stone.

Mr Ridgeway gasped. "The Ridgeway Ruby! I've not seen that for years."

Jerry frowned in concentration for a moment and then recalled the portrait of Helena Ridgeway looking pensively at a lily which she was holding in her long, white fingers. One of them was adorned with a large ruby.

Mr Ridgeway's eyes were misty. "My mother wore that and I gave it to Kate when we were married but your mother never had it, Jerry. Why not?"

Clare hesitantly interrupted to explain how she had found it but she said nothing of the letter. The old gentleman had felt enough emotion for one day. Jerry would know when to tell him of that.

The captain lifted her left hand and slid the ring on to her third finger. "It's your turn to wear it but I'll get you a sapphire as well — more suitable for a sailor's wife."

"Are you sure I ought to have it?"

"Don't be silly, my dear. It's yours now as it should be." Mr Ridgeway blew his nose vigorously.

Fortunately, Mrs Smith entered then and confessed that she didn't like the smell of the fish she had bought at Billingsgate and that the cat had drunk all the cream. The old gentleman's mood switched from sentiment to disgust. He swore at Jerry for not employing a good cook and subsequently stumped into dinner, leaning on the lieutenant's arm and declaring that his digestion would be ruined.

Clare followed behind, her fingers resting on the crook of the captain's arm. Jerry's eyes danced as he muttered to her, "It sounds an unappetising dinner but the old gentleman will grow bored with it. I can take him back to his hotel and then we can return to 'all that sloppy cuddling'."

THE END

NURSE ALICE IN LOVE
Theresa Charles

Accepting the post of nurse to little Fernie Sherrod, Alice Everton could not guess at the romance, suspense and danger which lay ahead at the Sherrod's isolated estate.

POIROT INVESTIGATES
Agatha Christie

Two things bind these eleven stories together — the brilliance and uncanny skill of the diminutive Belgian detective, and the stupidity of his Watson-like partner, Captain Hastings.

LET LOOSE THE TIGERS
Josephine Cox

Queenie promised to find the long-lost son of the frail, elderly murderess, Hannah Jason. But her enquiries threatened to unlock the cage where crucial secrets had long been held captive.

TIGER TIGER
Frank Ryan

A young man involved in drugs is found murdered. This is the first event which will draw Detective Inspector Sandy Woodings into a whirlpool of murder and deceit.

CAROLINE MINUSCULE
Andrew Taylor

Caroline Minuscule, a medieval script, is the first clue to the whereabouts of a cache of diamonds. The search becomes a deadly kind of fairy story in which several murders have an other-worldly quality.

LONG CHAIN OF DEATH
Sarah Wolf

During the Second World War four American teenagers from the same town join the Army together. Forty-two years later, the son of one of the soldiers realises that someone is systematically wiping out the families of the four men.

THE LISTERDALE MYSTERY
Agatha Christie

Twelve short stories ranging from the light-hearted to the macabre, diverse mysteries ingeniously and plausibly contrived and convincingly unravelled.

TO BE LOVED
Lynne Collins

Andrew married the woman he had always loved despite the knowledge that Sarah married him for reasons of her own. So much heartache could have been avoided if only he had known how vital it was to be loved.

ACCUSED NURSE
Jane Converse

Paula found herself accused of a crime which could cost her her job, her nurse's reputation, and even the man she loved, unless the truth came to light.

THE PLEASURES OF AGE
Robert Morley

The author, British stage and screen star, now eighty, is enjoying the pleasures of age. He has drawn on his experiences to write this witty, entertaining and informative book.

THE VINEGAR SEED
Maureen Peters

The first book in a trilogy which follows the exploits of two sisters who leave Ireland in 1861 to seek their fortune in England.

A VERY PAROCHIAL MURDER
John Wainwright

A mugging in the genteel seaside town turned to murder when the victim died. Then the body of a young tearaway is washed ashore and Detective Inspector Lyle is determined that a second killing will not go unpunished.

DEATH ON A
HOT SUMMER NIGHT
Anne Infante

Micky Douglas is either accident-prone or someone is trying to kill him. He finds himself caught in a desperate race to save his ex-wife and others from a ruthless gang.

HOLD DOWN A SHADOW
Geoffrey Jenkins

Maluti Rider, with the help of four of the world's most wanted men, is determined to destroy the Katse Dam and release a killer flood.

THAT NICE MISS SMITH
Nigel Morland

A reconstruction and reassessment of the trial in 1857 of Madeleine Smith, who was acquitted by a verdict of Not Proven of poisoning her lover, Emile L'Angelier.

SEASONS OF MY LIFE
Hannah Hauxwell
and Barry Cockcroft

The story of Hannah Hauxwell's struggle to survive on a desolate farm in the Yorkshire Dales with little money, no electricity and no running water.

TAKING OVER
Shirley Lowe and Angela Ince

A witty insight into what happens when women take over in the boardroom and their husbands take over chores, children and chickenpox.

AFTER MIDNIGHT STORIES,
The Fourth Book Of

A collection of sixteen of the best of today's ghost stories, all different in style and approach but all combining to give the reader that special midnight shiver.

DEATH TRAIN
Robert Byrne

The tale of a freight train out of control and leaking a paralytic nerve gas that turns America's West into a scene of chemical catastrophe in which whole towns are rendered helpless.

THE ADVENTURE OF THE CHRISTMAS PUDDING
Agatha Christie

In the introduction to this short story collection the author wrote "This book of Christmas fare may be described as 'The Chef's Selection'. I am the Chef!"

RETURN TO BALANDRA
Grace Driver

Returning to her Caribbean island home, Suzanne looks forward to being with her parents again, but most of all she longs to see Wim van Branden, a coffee planter she has known all her life.

SKINWALKERS
Tony Hillerman

The peace of the land between the sacred mountains is shattered by three murders. Is a 'skinwalker', one who has rejected the harmony of the Navajo way, the murderer?

A PARTICULAR PLACE
Mary Hocking

How is Michael Hoath, newly arrived vicar of St. Hilary's, to meet the demands of his flock and his strained marriage? Further complications follow when he falls hopelessly in love with a married parishioner.

A MATTER OF MISCHIEF
Evelyn Hood

A saga of the weaving folk in 18th century Scotland. Physician Gavin Knox was desperately seeking a cure for the pox that ravaged the slums of Glasgow and Paisley, but his adored wife, Margaret, stood in the way.

DEAD SPIT
Janet Edmonds

Government vet Linus Rintoul attempts to solve a mystery which plunges him into the esoteric world of pedigree dogs, murder and terrorism, and Crufts Dog Show proves to be far more exciting than he had bargained for . . .

A BARROW IN THE BROADWAY
Pamela Evans

Adopted by the Gordillo family, Rosie Goodson watched their business grow from a street barrow to a chain of supermarkets. But passion, bitterness and her unhappy marriage aliented her from them.

THE GOLD AND THE DROSS
Eleanor Farnes

Lorna found it hard to make ends meet for herself and her mother and then by chance she met two men — one a famous author and one a rich banker. But could she really expect to be happy with either man?

THE SONG OF THE PINES
Christina Green

Taken to a Greek island as substitute for David Nicholas's secretary, Annie quickly falls prey to the island's charms and to the charms of both Marcus, the Greek, and David himself.

GOODBYE DOCTOR GARLAND
Marjorie Harte

The story of a woman doctor who gave too much to her profession and almost lost her personal happiness.

DIGBY
Pamela Hill

Welcomed at courts throughout Europe, Kenelm Digby was the particular favourite of the Queen of France, who wanted him to be her lover, but the beautiful Venetia was the mainspring of his life.

PREJUDICED WITNESS
Dilys Gater

Fleur Rowley finds when she leaves London for her 'author's retreat' in the wilds of North Wales that she is drawn, in spite of herself, into an old tragedy.

GENTLE TYRANT
Lucy Gillen

Working as Ross McAdam's secretary, Laura couldn't imagine why his bitchy ex-wife should see her as a rival.

DEAR CAPRICE
Juliet Gray

Clifford Fortune married Caprice but his brother, Luke, knew the marriage was a mistake. He could allow himself to love Caprice blindly but that would be betraying his own brother.

IN PALE BATTALIONS
Robert Goddard

Leonora Galloway has waited all her life to learn the truth about her father, slain on the Somme before she was born, the truth about the death of her mother and the mystery of an unsolved wartime murder.

A DREAM FOR TOMORROW
Grace Goodwin

In her new position as resident nurse at Coombe Magna, Karen Stevens has to bear the emnity of the beautiful Lisa, secretary to the doctor-on-call.

AFTER EMMA
Sheila Hocken

Following the author's previous auto-biographies — EMMA & I, and EMMA & Co., she relates more of the hilarious (and sometimes despairing) antics of her guide dogs.

LEAVE IT TO THE HANGMAN
Bill Knox

Dope, dynamite, guns, currency — whatever it was John Kilburn and his son Pat had known how to get it in or out of England, if the price was right. But their luck changed when one of them killed a cop.

A VIOLENT END
Emma Page

To Chief Inspector Kelsey there was no shortage of suspects when Karen Boland was murdered, and that was before he discovered that she stood to inherit substantially at twenty-one.

SILENCE IN HANOVER CLOSE
Anne Perry

In 1884 Robert York is found brutally murdered at his home in Hanover Close. When, three years later, Inspector Pitt is asked to investigate, the murder remains unsolved.

A RARE BENEDICTINE
Ellis Peters

Three vintage tales of medieval intrigue and treachery featuring the author's monastic sleuth Brother Cadfael.

POIROT'S EARLY CASES
Agatha Christie

In this collection of eighteen stories, Hercule Poirot begins his celebrated career in crime.

THE SILVER LINK
— THE SILKEN LIE
Lynn Granger

Elspeth is determined to preserve her Scottish heritage and the Elliot name, but running Everanlea, a large hill farm, presents problems.

DOM

Library at Home Service
Community Services
Hounslow Library, CentreSpace
24 Treaty Centre, High Street
Hounslow TW3 1ES

YOUR COMMUNITY
YOUR SERVICES

0	1	2	3	4	5	6	7	8	9
970	532			634	491	536		818	419
	7731			704	748	116			638
	644	33		6414	565	726	712		
		92				316	3093		
		943			7636	3087			
		3182			346	507			
7927					706				

P10-L-2061

✓